The Missing Woman
and Other Stories

T0099268

Carole Burns is an author and lecturer who lives in Cardiff. Her book based on interviews with writers, *Off the Page: Writers Talk About Beginnings, Endings and Everything in Between*, was published by Norton in 2008. She regularly interviews authors and reviews books for *The Washington Post*, and her stories have appeared in *Ploughshares* and *Puerto del Sol*. She is Head of Creative Writing at the University of Southampton and a co-organizer of XX Woman's Writing Festival. *The Missing Woman* is her first collection of stories.

www.caroleburns.com

The Missing Woman
and Other Stories

Carole Burns

Parthian, Cardigan SA43 1ED
www.parthianbooks.com
First published in 2015
© Carole Burns 2015
ISBN 978-1-910409-66-4
Editor: Susie Wild
Cover design by Torben Schacht
Front cover image: "dress me" by Linnea Larsson, www.scanpix.com
Typeset by Elaine Sharples
Printed and bound in the US by Edwards Brothers Malloy
Published with the financial support of the Welsh Books Council
British Library Cataloguing in Publication Data
A cataloguing record for this book is available from the British Library.

To Dad,
and, belatedly, Mom,
for keeping our house full of books

Contents

The Missing Woman

Jill felt the baby breathing sleep into her arms as she watched the mechanic hoist her bicycle onto a lift. The gears were noisy, shifting before she did. The mechanic turned her wheels to listen – quick *click-click-click*s like a stream over rocks – heard the gears shift, shifted them himself. He reached behind him, without looking, to grasp a wrench with his right hand, tossed it lightly to his left, as if it were a girl on his arm, then stepped forward to stop the spinning wheel with the palm of his hand, all of it – Jill, the bike, baby Trina, the shop – suspended by his gentle motion.

"Hey, what's wrong with it?" Her husband strode into the shop holding their daughter April's hand. She was silent as she walked, thumb in her mouth, still not fully awake after falling asleep in the car. He had on his Saturday voice, the voice Jill hoped to hear when she woke in the morning – cheery, friendly, open to the day. His job as a prosecutor had been snapped shut in his briefcase or maybe tossed in the shed where Michael kept his tools. Jill didn't care where, as long as it had disappeared.

"Just needs a little adjustment," said the mechanic, maybe also the shop owner. He was thin – tall and thin with grainy blond hair so sandy it was nearly grey, no sheen at all. He

1

had that proprietary air about him, comfortable among the bikes and the tools he seemed to find by feel.

It was Michael who'd wanted Jill's bike tweaked on their way to Georgetown to ride the Canal Trail. Though she was anxious to get on the trail, she had indulged him. She liked the idea of stopping in Dupont Circle for a quick tune-up the way they used to on weekend mornings before the girls were born, with just themselves and their bikes and maybe a bottle of water.

"It's an old bike," Jill said apologetically. Though its body still gleamed blue, its silver gears were mottled black, in places even rusty. Michael had been after her for years to get a new one.

"It's a beaut," the man said. "Parts all made of metal – not plastic. Bikes are lighter these days, but cheaper too."

She raised her eyebrows at Michael, gave him a little "Ha!" He swung April's hand into one of his, then the other. His body was thick and softly muscular, almost plush. He was barely taller than Jill; their gazes were completely even.

"You think you've won now, don't you," he said lightly, the Southern accent that re-emerged sporadically, when he was sleepy, when he was home in Atlanta, coming through.

"You hitting the trails?" The mechanic pulled the chains loose from the gears. In his hands, the metal links looked elastic.

"We're going to drive down to Georgetown, take off from there." She described their route – taking the Capital Crescent trail until it intersected with the canal, following the dirt towpath as far as they dared with the girls in tow. Michael used to prefer the paved efficiency of the Capital Crescent – had liked getting lunch at one of the restaurants where it ended in downtown Bethesda. Now, he had decided the Canal

Trail was wider, flatter, less crowded, and therefore safer for the kids. Jill took this small gift gladly. She liked looking left to the river, right toward the canal, as if she were floating between two bodies of water.

"I have a favorite spot," she said, shifting Trina carefully to her other shoulder. The baby squirmed but didn't wake. "Near Lock 7. I go there in the mornings when Michael can watch the kids. When I'm able to rouse myself out of bed early enough. I've seen black-crowned night herons there. Green herons. And of course blues."

Michael pulled April to his leg, cupped his hand on the side of her head and stood, straight and alert.

"I know that spot," the mechanic said. "It's near Little Falls."

"That's right! Do you go? I've always wanted to get there at dawn – haven't made it yet." They chattered on about routes, favorite mini-trails that went down to the river, where Jill would get off her bike, walk through the trees and brush to sit and watch the water.

As the bike guy went in back to get a part, Jill grazed her cheek on Trina's baby hair, her warm head. She closed her eyes and remembered the last time she'd been able to get out at dawn before Michael went to work, the feeling of weightlessness as she took off on her own, of danger, even, as she slipped through Michael's overprotective worry. It was probably two months ago now; it had been only the second or third warm day of spring. She gazed around the shop and found Michael staring at her with snap-black eyes.

"You shouldn't spill your life out to strangers," he said.

She stood still, held Trina, tried not to wake her. She whispered fiercely. "Michael!"

"Freaking giving him your minute-by-minute itinerary." He

lifted April to his hip, but she wriggled down. He kept hold of her hand as she tried to escape to run around the shop. "You just shouldn't."

"Everyone uses those trails! He's not an axe murderer."

The mechanic returned as Trina was beginning to fuss herself awake. Jill wrapped her arms around her and swayed in place. The world, she thought, wasn't a crime scene. But she kept quiet. Maybe she had been talking too much, because the bike mechanic didn't speak either. He stepped to the front of the bike, spun the wheel, lifted the chain off, reached back for a tool, listening, concentrating only on his work. Jill knew from his fluid movements that he'd be a good dancer. His touch was light yet attentive, his lead just that – a lead, not a push, so light you felt you were leading, the same way he let the bike lead while guiding it just the same. He was probably gay, a thin dancing bike mechanic in Dupont Circle, so Jill let herself imagine dancing with him, his hand on her waist, his movements graceful. She could almost feel him guiding her as she held her baby daughter close, her husband, dark, stocky, by her side.

* * *

At the head of the trail, Michael assembled what Jill had taken to calling their *royal entourage* – a name that annoyed him slightly. He knew she was poking fun at both of them, at how huge a family of four seemed these days. But he also felt it was directed at him – his insistence on the right equipment (*paraphernalia*, Jill called it, like it was a spoon or a straw in a drug case, and she had to make it sound incriminating.) As Jill settled with the girls in the shade, he took their bikes off the car rack. Worried he might have dislodged the repairs made at the shop, he spun her wheel, heard with satisfaction the greased silence of chain over gears. At least now it seemed workable.

The baby seat came next. Here he'd spared no expense, though Jill had prevented him from buying the very top of the line. He hooked it to the back of his bike. Of course the man at the shop had to back her up on that old bike of hers— he probably made more money doing repairs than by selling a new one. When he wasn't luring women to share their favorite places to bike alone. He imagined Jill laying her bike in the weeds, walking to the river, unaware of the shadow of a man lurking behind a tree. Michael flushed, embarrassed, a little ashamed, but angry too. He'd have to make a joke of it later, let Jill know he was sorry. Though he wasn't, entirely.

He began to assemble their newest attachment, the trailer for April that wheeled along behind his bike. Jill gave everything a name, and this had several: April's covered wagon, go-cart, bubble-cart, red caboose. He took pleasure in setting things up just right. He lost himself in the unfolding of the nylon tent, the fitting of tent over cart, the snapping of metal clips over bolts. It made him feel he could protect this world – this still-new world of diapers and feedings and inexplicable tears.

At home, he'd been able to handle just one child, felt confident that all his and Jill's attention would be enough. Two was different. Everything – breakfast, dinner, the house, the simple task of getting out the door – was difficult. He'd get home at night to disorder. Sometimes he loved it, the very unpredictability of whether fish sticks were okay that night, what word April might bring home from playgroup like a toy. Other times, he'd put off going home, hoping that by the time he arrived the turmoil might be over. It never was. Trina would be squealing in a bath or fussing while getting fed, April throwing food on the floor for the dog. Except those nights he got home so late the house was dark and silent, Jill, Trina, April all asleep. The only light a small green lamp by the door. And then he'd miss it. Had Trina gone down okay? Which story did April have read to her? He'd regret missing every bit of it.

This morning was one of those May mornings that felt like summer in the sun, like spring in the shade. Behind him, near the boathouse, a few kayakers were carrying their crafts into the Potomac River. He wished again he could buy a kayak, even two – a single so they could each go out alone, a double for family trips. He liked being out in the water, soft waves thwacking against the boat, swans and geese and, once, in Cape Cod, a seal, swimming beside him as if he were a natural part of the river. A few miles up the canal, the government was renting out a stone lock house in exchange for upkeep. He'd almost asked Jill if she wanted to try it – become a citizen of all this.

He heard Trina fussing, across the trail, on the spot in the grass Jill had pitched herself and the girls. Baby must be getting hungry.

"Michael?" Jill called. Or had she been nursing Trina, right there? The only person she was hidden from was Michael, his view blocked by a Port-a-John. Every biker and hiker could see her as they rolled by.

"April coming your way!" Jill said.

She stuck out her head, looking right then left then right again for trail traffic, her hand on April's back, ready to give her a nudge. April hunched over like a little runner, ready to go.

Really— couldn't she wait a second? "Hon, let me come get her!"

A quick opening, and Jill tapped April. "Sweetie— Go!" April hesitated, then ran her awkward toddler run, thighs rubbing against each other. She had his body, not Jill's lanky one, and his dark hair.

"Good girl!" he said as she arrived breathless and sweaty in his arms. "You gonna help Daddy?" With April there he would need more time, making sure she wasn't taking away bolts and nuts, explaining what he was doing. He didn't mind. She reminded him of his sister, who used to watch him assemble Erector sets and model planes, asking him a thousand questions until he'd yell at her, tell her he couldn't concentrate, then regret it afterward, the model less interesting without an audience.

Finally he had it all put together – bikes, baby seat, trailer – and they set off, Michael in front, Jill taking up the rear. Despite Jill's protests, he hooked the baby seat and the trailer to his bike, and let Jill ride unencumbered. He liked tugging the weight of both girls, liked Jill having all of them in sight. She stuck closer to him than she would have pre-kid, when she used to coast behind at her own pace, looking for deer, pointing out turtles, then suddenly dash ahead of him as if he'd been going too slowly all along. As she kept close behind him he felt in command for the first time in months, free of worry – the baby tucked in back, April safe in her red, covered wagon, Jill tight behind him. They sailed along in a world he could handle.

* * *

Ahead, two women wearing pants and jean jackets, as if it were cold out, were halting people on the trail. A younger woman, long black hair slipping forward in greeting, held out a friendly hand when she approached people; the other, older, with silvery blond hair, stood back. They stuck out as incongruous. Political petition? Jill thought. Here on the trail? Some people whizzed by on their bikes without slowing down. Even from a distance it looked rude and Jill resolved at least to stop and hear what they wanted.

"I'm sorry to bother you." The younger woman, carrying flyers, smiled in apology. Her face was pale as winter. "We're looking for our friend. She's been missing since Tuesday."

Since Tuesday? Jill counted the days as she and Michael stood astride their bikes. She'd been missing for five days! The woman's sing-song voice nearly lulled the menace right out of what she was saying. Was her friend even alive? Why hadn't they read about this in the paper?

The woman continued. "We think she might have been here. Here on the trail."

"Why do you think she was here?" Michael asked, sharp.

"Her car was found in the neighborhood back there—" she motioned behind her— "right near the trail. We think maybe she'd parked and taken a walk. But—" She hesitated for the first time. "We don't really know."

The friend handed them a flyer with the woman's photo. She'd been caught by surprise, a smile just beginning to appear, blond hair loose around her face; she looked pretty in a casual sort of way.

"So were you here on the trail, Tuesday morning?" The first woman asked. "Have you seen anything?"

"No," Michael answered for them. "We mainly come on weekends. Jill used to come in the mornings." He made it sound like past tense. "Was she a jogger? Did she take morning walks?"

"Mommy, Mommy," April started chanting from her trailer.

"Honey, shush."

"Not really." The woman's voice sounded matter-of-fact, a forced, practiced calm as if she'd been doing this her whole life. Jill wondered when it would hit them – how many separate times it would hit them that their friend was missing.

"Mommy, Mommy, Mommy." Faster and louder.

Michael was in prosecutor mode, gentle with his soft accent, but firm. "Where exactly was her car? Were her keys in it? Did she know anyone in the area? Do you think she could have gotten on the Ride-On bus to the Metro?" Jill used to like this Michael. He used to make her feel safe, like he'd get all the information they needed. Today, she just wished he'd back down.

The woman on the flyer stared back at Jill, her eyebrow raised as if in a challenge. She looked bemused, as if all of this – as if life – were slightly funny. Jill tried to figure out if she'd seen her on the trail, on the few days she was able to get out on her own. Would she remember her? She might be more likely to recall someone's golden retriever, a limpy jog, than her face or hair.

"Did she take walks in the morning?" Michael asked. "Are you sure she was here, on the trail?"

"Listen—" The second woman, shorter, stepped forward and spoke for the first time. She was wiry and tensely athletic – someone who, restless at dawn, might go hiking the trail. "Listen, I'm her sister, and I don't even know. But thanks for stopping."

No one said anything as the sister stood, hand on her hip, ready to move on. It was as if the missing woman herself had shown up to plead her case. Jill looked at the photo for a resemblance and recognized the woman's demanding gaze. "Good luck," Jill said as she found her voice. "I wish we'd seen her. That we'd been here."

Michael turned to grab his handlebars, but Jill remained still. Ahead, on the trail, she saw that strong vines growing from the canal had already tentacled onto the dirt towpath. The woods across the canal, the swampy undergrowth between the trail and the river, the trail itself – all seemed vast and impenetrable. How would they ever find her? Then the river and the canal, which should have made the search seem easier – limiting the land to a thin strip – themselves became menacing, as if they could swallow up all of them, let alone one woman, missing for five days.

"Yeah, good luck," Michael added.

"Can we help?" Jill asked. It popped out of her mouth as she thought of how thick the growth would get as the summer went on. Did the sister know? By July, it would feel like a jungle.

"Mommy, Mommy, Mommy!"

She could sense Michael stiffen, though he released his handlebars, smiled pleasantly.

"I mean, can we help you look for her?" Jill asked. "Do you have enough people looking?"

The women hesitated. The young one glanced at Trina and April. "Sure, but—"

The sister finished. "You've got a full boat today."

Michael stuck out his hand, wished them luck again, and ended the conversation without seeming as if he'd cut anything short, though Jill knew he had – he had cut her short from volunteering the whole family, from turning their bike ride into a search for a woman they didn't know. She thought about saying something as the women walked away but didn't.

"You really shouldn't be biking this alone," he said, his foot on his pedal. April was quiet as she sensed they were setting off again.

"We don't even know she was on the trail," Jill said.

He took off. She looked back at the women halting two walkers, answering questions although they didn't have much information to share, didn't know why their friend and sister was missing, what she'd been doing, where she had been. *Was she a jogger? I'm sorry. Good luck.* Jill got on her bike and caught up to Michael, Trina, April – the royal entourage. She didn't look back again to see.

* * *

Michael felt himself riding faster than normal. He slowed down, then began thinking again of the woman – missing for five days already? she didn't stand a chance – and knew his legs were pumping faster again. April's cart rattled loudly over a small pothole. Would Jill really have stopped to help? Did she realize this is what he did every day, help people determine what happened to husbands, brothers, sisters who were killed, abused? Did she?

Yesterday he had watched the faces of the grand jurors listen in their objective juror masks to the testimony of a five-year-old boy, his kid voice lilting high and summery in that dark chamber meant for adults. Describing what the man had done to him when his mother wasn't home. Naming parts of a body a boy shouldn't know the names of. Describing acts a boy shouldn't have even imagined yet. One juror held his hand over his eyes as if the boy's words were a light too harsh for the man to bear, so he hid his eyes because he couldn't block his ears.

It was a victory for Michael. The grand jury was so convinced they'd upped the charge to the more serious offense he had argued for, that he'd been told to back off from by his boss. A good day at the office. He'd watched the faces of the jurors not used to what he had heard a thousand times already – from this boy, from others. Maybe that's what scared him – knowing too much, being inured to it, not trusting himself to be careful enough, so he was too careful.

He found Jill in his rearview mirror. She was nearly anonymous under her bike helmet and sunglasses but still feminine, with her slim arms, her tight breasts a little larger since she was still nursing. He wished there was a way to make her look more like a man when she was out here riding by herself. Her long hair, already back in a ponytail, could be pinned up. She could wear a looser shirt. Because she looked so female despite her slim tomboy frame. He'd buy her an iPhone for Christmas, though she didn't want one, didn't want any more gadgets. *It's disgusting how many gadgets Americans buy that they don't need.* No, not for Christmas, he'd just upgrade to the next version and give her his iPhone, justify it that way, turn on that app that lets you locate the phone when it's lost. He'd always be able to find her.

"Michael, wait."

Jill braked, skidding on the sand. He stopped gently, then turned toward her without getting off his bike. What was the problem? Trina gurgled behind him as if the mere sight of his face gave her joy.

"Michael, I want to help them. Can't we help them?"

He heard himself sigh. He tried to sound patient, reasonable. "Jill, we've got two kids here. Sweetie, we're already behind schedule. The girls are going to be hungry pretty soon—" His reasons sounded stupid and selfish. He felt stupid and selfish but he didn't want to stop. He didn't think it was the responsible thing to do. Besides, the search was pointless – a necessary gesture, but largely pointless. He tried to say the next part gently. "Honey, their friend – her sister – probably isn't alive. It's been five days." Was he the only one who realized this?

"How can we not help them? We're not doing anything…"

He wondered what the woman's friends thought they were accomplishing; he could see they weren't doing a good job. They should be bunched together, shoulder to shoulder, meticulously searching each square inch for clues – an earring, a button – instead of spreading out into groups of two or three as if they'd been scattered by the wind. They would need another fifty people to make a difference.

"Two more people, Jill, aren't going to help."

She was being impractical. She always was impractical, charmingly impractical, but she couldn't do that anymore and he was getting angry – she couldn't have her bike breaking down when they had two kids to get home, they couldn't drop their plans and join a search party with the girls in tow. Could they? She had to be more sensible. At the least, the kids would get hungry, tired, let alone upset if – God forbid – they found something. Jill would get upset. They would sense the atmosphere. Hell, he didn't want to be the one, beating back the thick brush off the trail, to discover, underneath a lush green fern, a woman's dead body.

"Honey, what if we find something? Do you want April seeing that? Living with that? Jill?"

* * *

Jill felt bombarded by Michael's logic, as if each fact was a little stone he was tossing at her bike helmet. He was right but he wasn't right. How could they not stop?

"We used to help," she said.

13

She threw that at him, that maybe just a few years ago they would have stopped and helped. Jill would have – on her own she would have done it without thinking. She used to carry Michael along on these impulses of hers. He'd join her as if they were doing something crazy – bungee-jumping, parachuting. He'd step up with a sense of adventure.

"We didn't have any kids, hon. We have more than ourselves to worry about now."

Jill thought about the girls and their hunger and felt her right breast, the one Trina preferred, suddenly full, brimming. It spilled wet into the cup of her nursing bra. But she'd just eaten. Trina should be fine.

"She'll be fine," Jill said. "They'll be—"

A biker raced toward them. He whizzed by in a flash of yellow nylon, black helmet, tanned arms, legs pedaling so fast they were almost spiraling. And then he was gone. She smelled his sweat, subtle and strange. She didn't know what to make of them – the men like machines on their bikes, the women walking, the couples jogging with their happy dogs, all of them oblivious to the missing woman and Jill and her daughters who were bound to be hungry or tired or frightened.

"Oh, Michael," she said.

She heard his kickstand clink against a rock and his sneakers on the dirt as he walked to her. Her bike was still under her as he hugged her, almost tipping them. "It's frightening, isn't it?" He kissed her forehead like he would one of the kids'. "It's horrible."

She wanted to believe it, that she was crying over a woman she didn't know.

"You come here by yourself. It's frightening." She felt her tears wetting his shirt. "Do you want to go look for her? We can look for her. The kids won't know. I'm sorry."

She looked up at him and saw that he meant it. She knew he didn't want to stop and search, even now. Most people wouldn't think of stopping; most women with two children and a husband they didn't see enough anymore wouldn't even consider bringing two children, when those kids were just about ready to eat, on a search party. The idea itself was an extravagance. Jill felt herself relent.

"No— it's OK. The kids…" she said.

"You sure?" he asked. She could hear the relief in his voice. But he said it kindly – he meant it.

April howled. The sound was dulled by the nylon cover of her wagon – but still loud. Jill ran over to her – it didn't sound like a hurt scream – and peered inside. A scared scream? April's face was already red as if she'd been crying for hours, not seconds, her cheeks completely wet. "Honey, come here. What is it, Sweetie?" April crawled out of the wagon to be held, soothed. Michael patted her head as Jill held her. They walked over to Trina— a pre-emptive strike. She looked worried, or maybe just curious. Jill was still amazed that one didn't always set off the other. April quieted in her arms.

"What was that?" Michael asked, tempting fate— they couldn't assume her crying fit was over.

"Maybe tired. Hungry." Jill asked her daughter but April couldn't say; she wasn't old enough yet to put words to whatever was making her cry. Jill wondered if anyone was. They gave both their girls apple juice and graham crackers, then prepared to set off again. "I wonder if she just wanted to be moving," she said. They laughed at the idea – their imperious toddler, demanding the royal entourage get rolling again.

* * *

Ahead of her, April and Trina seemed content. Their heads turned one way, then another, as joggers and rollerbladers and bicyclists sped at them and past them. She could see the red shadow of April inside her wagon, her back completely straight. Ever since she could sit up, April had held herself erect, like a dancer. On the river, a crew team rounded markers for a practice run. A pair of kayaks – one yellow, one red – glided downstream. In rhythm, their paddles flashed in the sun.

Michael's bell *ching-ching*ed as he passed a pair of walkers. A muscle twitched under his nylon shirt. He held his back straight, barely turning to look at the river or the canal, interested only in going forward. As she followed him, she wondered, for a moment, if he still loved her. As he pedaled swiftly on, relieved to be going again, relieved her fit of willfulness was over, she felt this piece of him resisting her – steel-like, unyielding. Of course he loved her – she knew he did – but she didn't know it the way she used to, in a wave of knowing that stayed within her, never left but kept gently insisting as if she'd always known. Now she knew with her head – of course he loved her – first with her head before she could feel it in her heart.

She also knew she'd regret not stopping – all day and all night and all weekend and years later, if she thought of it, she'd regret not stopping to help search for the missing woman. She wondered if her regret over not stopping would make her stop the next time. And she knew it wouldn't, and her regret turned inward, as she wondered what was missing, why she wouldn't be able to stop, why the kids and Michael and the fear of not being able to keep her family whole made her unable to follow her instinct to reach out.

for Alison

Honour's Daughter

Martin Honour, an ache in his throat, watched his sixteen-year-old daughter perched over the edge of the pool. This was the only place he saw her body – all eighty-eight and one-quarter pounds of it this week – usually hidden in oversized sweaters and jeans baggier than the style. Even here, Liza concealed herself in a thick, white robe until seconds before she had to get on her mark. She did her warm-ups in her robe, stretching and bending like some animate towel— so Martin Honour was shocked to see her emerge from that fulsome whiteness like a butterfly without her wings.

She balanced on the edge of the pool, her arms bracing behind her sinewy, even strong. The rest of her was almost skeletal – legs so thin they bowed out at the knees, hips that stuck out of her bathing suit like holsters, her torso so frail it was almost misshapen, bent slightly to the right.

Honour was surprised she could swim at all – that the weight of the water and the force of the other girls' kicks didn't push her floating to its surface like a stick – for surely, if people weigh less in water, then Liza ought to weigh next to nothing.

The buzzer catapulted the girls into the water and Honour to his feet; he beat the start of bubbling kicks, was standing while the swimmers still glided through their dives. Honour was a bit of a joke at the meets, the only bystander almost falling off the bleachers in his excitement. Parents and teachers liked to point him out. "Look— there's the superintendent of schools." Screaming into the heavy, humid air – "C'mon Liza! You can do it! C'mon, girl!" – Honour tried with his raspy voice to give her more energy, to give her more strength.

She moved forward steadily, a quiet, efficient jet of white water trailing after her, six times up and down the pool – a middle-distance race, since she had neither the power for a sprint nor the stamina for anything longer. Some swimmers jumped ahead then lagged behind; others lagged behind then took the lead. Liza remained almost neutral. Even on the last leg, no matter how much Honour shouted and coaxed, Liza continued at the same purposeful pace. Honour suspected she didn't have enough energy left to sprint to the finish; he worried, sometimes, that she would not finish at all.

The swimmers slid off their bathing caps and goggles and hung on to the side of the pool, their large shoulders bulging into their necks as they waited for the times to be posted – all except Liza, who lay on her back in the water in an upside-down dead-man's float. When the times went up, she stood, water gleaming down her fragile neck. "All right!" Honour said. Liza had finished fourth – not enough to score any points for her team, but she had beaten her best time. She looked back for a moment toward the bleachers, and Honour, still standing, raised his arm in a thumb's up. He thought he saw her smile as she turned to hoist herself out of the pool.

It was Liza's only race that day – her doctor had limited her to one per meet – so Honour made his way to pool level, talking to parents and teachers as he went. He met her, cocooned again in her white robe, halfway between her bench and the stands.

"Great job, kiddo," he said.

"Thanks." Liza's pale face, usually framed protectively by her short, blond hair, was flushed from the race; her hair was slicked against her head from the water, dark and boyish-looking. She smiled more easily; she giggled, once or twice, like a teenager should.

"You beat your best by how much?" Honour asked.

"Almost two seconds."

He whistled low, which made her smile again, and they laughed.

"You don't have to hang around," she said. "Nance's mother can take me home."

Honour, with the hours he usually spent at the office Saturday mornings tugging at his conscience, should have been relieved. Instead, his feelings were hurt. "You sure?" he asked.

"Yeah, she already mentioned it," Liza said. "I know you have work to do."

"Well. Call me if you need a ride. I'll be at the office."

"Got it."

She watched him leave. He waved at a few people, bent down his sandy white head as he thanked Nancy's mother, then glided with long, smooth strides out the door. As he disappeared Liza felt faint, the moist warmth of the room, the sharp smell of chlorine, blending to overwhelm her. She stood there for a few moments, dizzy, wondering if she would fall. She felt as if the bright room were growing vaster, the high ceilings and gleaming walls moving farther and farther away. She could feel herself retreating, getting smaller, until she reached for the tile wall to steady herself. Her vision cleared. She joined her teammates on the bench.

* * *

"Don't you like life?" Honour asked.

"I guess," Liza said. "But— what's the point?"

They sat at the dining room table, never used anymore except for these discussions. Something about the dark, cherry length of it, the gleaming surface, the formality of the stiff chairs and the high, unlit tapers provided a refuge from the wreckage of life. In half-darkness, in the shadows of the kitchen light, Honour's lanky body re-folded into the chair like a grasshopper's, his right knee sticking over the table. His face was proportionately long and thin, a faint yellow that marks a squandered tan, with dry flecks of skin around his smile. His pale blue eyes, streaked with gray and darker blue, always challenged, waited to laugh, to think, to answer.

"What do you like about life?" Honour asked.

Liza spoke carefully, her hands clasped on the table. "I like being with my friends. I like— you. I like Mom, if she's sober, if she's here."

"If," he echoed quietly.

"I like not eating," she said.

"You like not eating?" He was genuinely surprised, at both the fact that her sickness somehow gave enjoyment, and that she admitted it.

"I like the hunger," Liza said. She sometimes wondered if she was emptying herself, leaving an outline, a sketch that she could then fill in with details, flesh out – or throw away. "But the hunger doesn't last," she added.

"That's abstaining from life – it's not life."

"Yes it is," she said. "I'm just taking it to extremes."

He decided not to argue with her, with this teenager turned forty by her wisdom, turned ten by her body. Had she always been this serious?

"What else?" he asked. "Do you like the soup kitchen?"

"Oh. It's okay."

"Well, that's enthusiastic," Honour said.

"I like the idea of the soup kitchen."

"You don't like going?"

"I feel phony and hypocritical when I go. Self-righteous."

"But you're not."

"But that's how I feel."

"You're being too hard on yourself," he said, yet he knew what she meant. If she could help at the soup kitchen without making an appearance – without others seeing her – that would be true goodness. "But it's important to go— to do that sort of thing."

"Why?" Liza asked.

"Why, why, why?" he echoed. Each "why" led back to her first question, her persisting question: Why do we live? Honour didn't know how to answer her. "It's childish to keep asking 'Why,'" he said.

"Why?"

"It's what three-year-olds do. The why stage. Don't touch the stove. Why? Because it will hurt you. Why? Because it's hot. Why? Because we're cooking. Why? Because we're hungry. Why? Because we haven't eaten in a while. Why? Because we just haven't! Eventually you reach a question that can't be answered. Or is too obvious to answer. Or drops you into a circle you can't escape."

"Why?" The joke didn't work. She so wanted to ask questions; she desperately wanted to know the answers.

* * *

Honour sat now at a different table, a table for two, so cramped his knees bumped Fran's whenever he moved them, and because of that, like a teenage boy on a date, he moved them often. Honour and Fran liked this small neighborhood restaurant, twenty miles from their homes. Everyone seemed to know everyone except them – which was, after all, exactly what Fran and Honour wanted. If the secrecy of their affair was inconvenient, it also made them feel more intimate. They were forced to hide out together, this boss and secretary; they were forced to be alone.

"At eighty-five pounds Liza goes into the hospital," Honour said. "Today she weighed eighty-seven and a third pounds. A third of a pound. It's like we're measuring saffron, for Christ's sake."

Fran took his long, dry hand, her palms moist on his, and massaged his knuckles with her thumb. He leaned toward her, her body made up of curves rather than angles. She reminded him of the comforting roundness of a loaf of homemade bread, the scent and color of wheat.

"Then I drop her off to volunteer at the soup kitchen. I mean – does she see the irony in that? Is that why she goes, because it's ironic? We talk about life. We talk about why. What's the point, Dad? Why bother? So I say, why not?"

"That's not enough," Fran said.

"What do you mean?"

"'Why not?' is not enough reason to live."

The waitress arrived with their meals, large bowls and plates that barely fit between them. Fran started to release her hand from Honour's, but he held on to it, softly tightening his grip, smiling at her. He was amazed at what could make her blush. It was always the small things, the barely noticeable displays of affection, perhaps because, overlooked by everyone else, they became intensely personal.

"I can't do this at the office, you know," he said after the waitress left, neither of them changing position to eat.

"Do you think the soup kitchen is for her mother?" Fran asked.

"Her mother?"

"Liza's going to know that a lot of homeless people are alcoholics."

"Christ – is that why?" Martin felt his face flush then he could barely catch his breath. Anger, he knew. The merest mention of his wife these days brought it on. How many years had that been building? "And of course she hasn't fucking phoned or written her daughter yet. Week Seven of rehab."

Fran prepared herself again for the awkward task of defending her lover's wife. "She's ill, Martin."

"Well, Goddammit, so is Liza!" He tossed his napkin across the table, the weakness of the gesture all the more maddening when he wanted thunder, when he wanted roaring lions. Fran sat as quiet as her comfort.

"I'm sorry," he said, wondering where she would take his apology, if she would store it in her memory, and bring it out when she needed it, or throw it back at him when he was sharp with her again, as he was bound to be. "I think the only thing that kept Liza out of the hospital today were a few pennies in her pocket."

He picked up his napkin again, smoothed it on his lap. "I keep wanting to tell her about you," he said.

"Should you?"

"I can't," he said. "I'm too afraid."

* * *

"You know," Honour said, "contemporary artists – or at least art theorists – say abstraction is a way of celebrating art.

Celebrating the paint and the colors and the texture and the beauty of art. Art for art's sake."

"Okay." Liza was intent, listening.

"How about life— for life's sake."

"Then we need to invent an abstract life."

Honour laughed, startled out of the dialogue he had mapped out beforehand, pleased in the midst of his worry, in his effort to seem casual. "I didn't think of that."

"Formless," she said. "Oblique. Pointless."

"Abstract art isn't pointless."

"You could argue that it is."

"You don't believe that," he said, squinting with annoyance.

Liza had seen her father's eyes glint with sarcasm, go gray with impatience. But not too often. She knew she was, by and large, a good daughter, and they tended to spoil each other. She indulged his love of intelligence by being witty and introspective; he indulged her need of approval by approving. She indulged his impatience by acting like an adult; he, in turn, treated her – almost – as an equal. Yet they could spend days gliding around each other in a moveable stalemate, refusing to acknowledge imperfection in the other, imperfection in themselves.

"Life for life's sake," Liza repeated.

"You breathe to luxuriate in breathing. You eat to taste the spiciness of red pepper, the silkiness of a peach, the sweetness of ginger. Maybe you abstain – occasionally – to feel hunger. You love for the pleasure of it."

"Sounds rather Epicurean."

"Not if the pleasure is given and received," Honour said. "You go to the soup kitchen not only because it's helping others, but because of the joy of giving. For the joy of it, not because you're a do-gooder."

"But then it's still selfish."

"You wouldn't feel selfish about something that gave you pleasure. You would appreciate the art of it. Art for art's sake."

"Who's Art?"

"You'd just do what made you happy," he said.

* * *

Liza stared at the compact, blue box in the medicine cabinet – dared not touch it – but became mesmerized as it swayed before her. In her mind, she could hear the scraping of cardboard, the rustle of papers as she searched for the razor blades hidden inside, could see them flashing white in the bright, shining bathroom, reflecting onto the walls, onto the floor, into her eyes. Leaning on the sink, she teetered, her arms bending like tulips in a storm. She jolted awake, still staring at the unopened box.

* * *

"There's sex," Honour said, grinning to hide his embarrassment. He thought he was prepared – he thought he was cool enough – to talk to his daughter about sex. Now he wasn't so sure. He shifted in his chair.

"You're telling me I should live for sex?" Liza asked, amused as she saw his blush, the pale pink of a girl's.

"I didn't say that," he said.

"What were you saying then?"

"That sex is something— worthwhile."

"Worthwhile?" Liza said. "Talk about the kiss of death."

"Okay, okay. What I mean is that it can be a wonderful, deeply felt, deeply connecting experience."

"Can be."

"It isn't always, of course," Honour said. "Connecting… connecting is the key. That doesn't have to be sexual. If you can… reach someone. By just saying the right word. By hearing. By seeing. Even trying can make life meaningful. But the failure to do it – the failure to try – is what can make it meaningless."

"So you try."

"I try."

"Do you think you reach people?" she asked.

"Do I?" he asked her. He wished she didn't have to ask. "You tell me."

* * *

Thick pea soup sloshed onto her thumbs as Liza carried a bowl to a customer at the soup kitchen. Most clients filed up as in a cafeteria, but a few were disabled and so their food was brought to them. Liza was surprised they actually served soup at the soup kitchen; she thought it was a phrase whose origins had long disappeared. She delivered the bowl, wiped her fingers clean on her apron and retrieved another meal. Liza sometimes wondered if she would be more useful in the office – filing or typing or keeping books – but she didn't want people to think she didn't like the clients.

Yet she kept feeling conspicuous at the soup kitchen, not for her designer jeans or college sweatshirt, its thickness cinched and folded in by a thin belt, but because she realized her clothes didn't really hide her weight – not here. She felt the stares of questioning eyes, asking, "So what's your problem?" knowing she shouldn't have problems in her suburban harbor with the elegant oak trees, the gentle slope of well-paved streets, the stately homes built around the time of the Revolutionary War, all as well-preserved as their residents. She wanted to apologize for her self-imposed illness; this was the only time her doctor's word for it – self-mutilation – took on any meaning. Amid the ragged problems of the soup kitchen, her illness seemed another sterile luxury.

A woman who was hunched in a wheelchair thanked Liza as she delivered the last bowl of pea soup.

"Can I get you something else?" Liza asked. "Water? Coffee? Bread?"

"Well, I think God has given me my fill right now," the woman said, smoothing her black, kinked hair behind her ears. "He's done good by me today. We'll see about tomorrow. And then," she stared, winking at Liza, "we'll see about the day after that. But I must say," she added as she picked up her spoon, "that I'm not so sure God's done okay by you."

Liza found it was a relief to have someone mention it, to have the burden of it, for a moment, shared. She noticed a few people sitting near the woman glance at Liza's waist, as skinny as an arm, yet she was oddly unembarrassed.

"You sick?" the woman asked.

Liza hesitated. "I guess."

"It's not cancer, is it?"

"No. It isn't."

"Well, that's good, at least," she said.

"Do you have cancer?" Liza asked.

"No. Me? I'm just crippled."

Liza nodded as if this answered all her questions. It was, in a way, all she needed to know, yet she kept wondering when the woman became crippled, how and why.

After lunch, she found the director, Margaret, in her office. Liza was enchanted by the play of light and dark on

Margaret's features, her black, meticulously carved eyebrows on her clear brown skin, the shine of her short but polished nails against her silky, generous fingers.

"Do you know how the woman at lunch today, the friendly one in the wheelchair, became disabled?" Liza asked.

"Mrs. Brooks?" Margaret's clear vibrato making music out of those few notes. "She's a complicated one. She used to be an alcoholic."

"Used to be?"

"Well, you're correct – an alcoholic must remember she's always an alcoholic."

It wasn't what Liza had been thinking.

"And maybe she still drinks at home. I don't know. But years ago, she used to come in here, drunk by noon. Never disruptive. But sometimes we couldn't let her in. Against policy. So one day she showed up in a wheelchair. Sober enough to join us for lunch. And she's been that that way ever since. I'm not sure there was anything physically wrong with her. But she drinks less."

God's been good to me today. Mrs. Brooks's words replayed in Margaret's soft tones. *I'm just crippled.* "Is that a cure?" Liza asked, her own voice crackling against the melody in her head. A pale ache was arching through Liza's bones, penetrating to her back, up her shoulders, into her neck, her head, the delicate bones of her cheeks. She lifted her hand to grip the doorframe but she couldn't find it, couldn't feel the cool ripples of the painted cement. She leaned against it, knees bending, body falling— before she woke, Margaret's cool hands on her neck. "Liza. Liza, dear."

* * *

"Maybe the goodness lasts. Lingers somewhere," Honour said.

"In history? In books?" Liza asked.

"In the ether."

"The ether? Dad, you're going transcendental on me."

"I'm serious," he said.

"You're making it up as you go along."

"I know," he chuckled. She always caught him. "But I'm serious."

"So where is it all?" Liza asked.

"The goodness?"

"Why don't I feel goodness all around me? Why don't I feel like I'm inhaling goodness? Why's it feel like it's all used up? Like there's never been any goodness?"

* * *

Liza tried listening to Nancy's chatter as they stood near their lockers during the six-minute break between fourth and fifth period, the first time they had seen each other since driving to school. Something about Michael, her latest crush, something about her math teacher Mr. Coffey, then Nancy was slamming her locker, waving as she left for class. "Hi, Liza." "Hi, Liza." A quick chorus of greetings as students rushed by. Amid this hum of life, Liza wore her thinness like a badge of honor. It was her silent protest. "I am not well," it said. "I am not going to pretend."

Liza lingered, searched on tiptoe for a pen in her top locker as she waited for Jeff to join her for their daily walk to Chemistry. "Hey there," he said, his low, languid voice surprising her even though she was expecting him. He glanced easily into her locker, smiling, thinking it was cute she couldn't see into it. "Need some help?"

Neither of them liked to hurry, though the trek from Liza's locker to their classroom was probably the longest trip one could take within their high school. They enjoyed the slow stroll through the emptying hallways, savored a sense of freedom as classroom doors clicked shut, tasted a feeling of superiority as underclassmen raced by them. Liza felt lighter and lighter as she and Jeff walked together. Her head just reached his shoulder, and occasionally he bent down solicitously to hear her talk.

"So, you going to Michael's party Saturday?" Jeff asked.

"Isn't everybody?" Liza asked, setting him up for their little joke.

"Who's everybody," Jeff answered, enjoying the pretense that their lives were the whole world, that there was nothing outside it.

"You know," he said, "if you'd like a ride, I'd be happy to pick you up. We can go to the party together."

Liza was conscious of her elbow almost grazing his shirt, of her ear near his shoulder, of the way his body leaned slightly toward her.

"You know, unless Nancy's already picking you up," he added, giving her an out, giving himself one.

"Let me check with her," Liza said, thinking, Can I abandon her? Is he just being nice?

* * *

"So why do you swim?" Honour asked.

"I don't know. I like being underwater."

"You like to compete?"

"Not particularly."

"You're addicted to chlorine."

"Probably."

30

"You like feeling in shape."

"A little."

"You like burning off the calories."

Liza stopped for a moment. "Is that what you think?"

"I never thought of it before."

"Honest?"

"Honest," he said. Yet something told him it was partly true. "You think you should be involved in a sport?"

"Maybe that's it," she said.

"That's the hardest thing to learn," Honour said.

"What is?"

"How not to do things you think you should."

"But some things you should do," Liza said.

"Very few." He crouched in his chair, afraid to move, afraid to speak. How should he say this? Should he say it at all? "I tell you one thing someone should be doing."

Silence.

"Your mother should be calling you. At least writing."

Liza felt blinded by the blue of his shirt.

"I think she's incapable of it," he said. "But she should be... in contact with you."

She sat breathless, waiting for words, for reasons.

"I'm sorry," he said, not sure if he was apologizing for his own silence, his inability to explain; her mother's silence; or Liza's, torn between understanding and not understanding, between forgiving and not forgiving.

* * *

"Hey, Fran." Liza peeked in the doorway to Honour's office.

"Why, Liza— how good to see you," Fran said. "Is your Dad expecting you?"

"No, I thought I'd just say hi. I got out of practice early." Fran never seemed to move quickly but already she was on the phone, buzzing Honour. She had a calmness that was comforting. Liza had never seen her rattled or impatient. If efficiency could be warm it was Fran.

"He'll be done in five minutes," Fran said, her voice like a thrush, slightly deep, with a tiny flutter in the throat. "Your Dad said you did well in your last meet."

"Well, better, at least," Liza said.

"Congratulations." Fran's voice dipped in "gra—" giving the word a sincerity it didn't usually have.

Honour's door opened. "Well, my dear." Fran looked up quickly. Liza noticed – took in the pretty picture of Fran for once becoming flustered, her shuffling of papers, her rapid glance up at Honour. "What a lovely surprise," he said.

* * *

"You're having an affair with Fran."

Honour walking into the bright kitchen, stopped for a moment, then continued. His pale face flushed; keys crashed onto the counter.

"Who said that?"

"You two. A guess."

Liza stood at the sink, the weak sun dipping below the picture window. She had been waiting for her father, had been devising a plan to trick him, to make him say something profound about love or fidelity, then to call his bluff – to accuse. Instead Liza felt as if he had called her bluff. Seeing his tired face ready to smile for her made her blurt out her discovery as if she were the one with a confession to make.

"I don't know if you can call it an affair," Honour said.

"I wonder what Mom would call it?"

"Your mother and I are separated, I don't—"

"Mom and I are separated too," Liza said. "She's in a hospital."

Honour sat down at the breakfast table, weakly; merely sitting was an effort. He leaned an elbow on the table, rested his forehead in his hand, fingers stretched along his brow. "A headache," Liza thought. "I'm a real headache."

"You think your mother will be hurt? Is that what's bothering you?" Honour asked.

"No." Liza wasn't sure what hurt.

"Then?"

"It's just so— banal. Fucking your secretary."

"Liza!" Honour lifted his head, put his arm down.

"I would hope you'd think of someone more— imaginative."

"Fran is more than a secretary," he said, then cringed at his double meaning. Liza didn't seize upon it. She was too busy trying to remember what she had wanted to say. Such as, Why did you lie to me? Why Fran? Why anyone? None of it coming out.

"I don't want her here, in the house," Liza said, wondering if she sounded like her mother.

"Have I brought her here?"

"Where do you go? What do you do together? Is it just sex? Where do you go for—"

"That's none of your business, Eliza Ann! I'm warning you!"

"Are you going to ground me? Send me to my room? Why are you falling back on nonsense like parental authority?"

"Because you're pissing me off!"

They stared at each other in the awful, white kitchen. What

was the point of this? Why couldn't she explain herself? What was there to explain?

"Why didn't you tell me?" she finally asked.

"I couldn't. How could I?"

"I'm an adult."

Honour laughed, abrupt and cheerless. "I know," he admitted.

* * *

Days later, Liza, cooking up a peace offering, still felt more angry than forgiving. Pasta, a jar of sauce from the gourmet shop, a salad. She added spices to the sauce, then mushrooms, knowing Honour liked mushrooms, knowing she didn't, throwing them in to spite someone. Winter-cold water from the tap ran over her fingers, over the lettuce. She chopped everything into tiny pieces – as if the smaller they were, the less filling, the less fattening. Precisely measured a quarter pound of pasta for Honour, an eighth for herself – more than she could probably eat. Set it all up in the dining room with place mats and wine goblets for water.

Honour was still too frustrated, too embarrassed to be more than polite. "You did a lot of chopping," he said, noticing the miniscule pieces of carrots, the tiny bits of tomato, glancing at the small mound of pasta on his plate. He finished quickly, sat silent for a few minutes, holding his fork limply in his hand.

"Liza, this was very nice. But— I need more food than this."

"Are you still hungry?" she asked, surprised.

"Am I still hungry? Have we eaten yet?"

"Oh." Liza giggled. "Sorry." Her face screwed up into a

frown as she began laughing, Honour joining her, relieved, the two of them shaking, eyes tearing, until Honour realized Liza's tears were genuine.

"Liza," he said, "I was just joking."

She nodded her head frantically. "—funny," she squeezed out, laughing for a second, yet she couldn't stop the tears.

Honour did not want to leave her so he patted his empty pocket for a handkerchief, reached for a napkin and sent a fork clattering to the floor, finally strode into the kitchen and back in four long steps. He handed her a wad of Kleenex. "Tissues," he said.

Liza pressed them to her eyes in one clump. "I don't understand," she said. Honour stared at her small fingers hiding her eyes.

"You mean Fran?" he asked. Liza wasn't sure what she meant, but she waited anyway; Fran was certainly part of it.

"Things just happened, Liza," Honour said. "You don't choose people. We reject people, but we don't choose them. It's not conscious. Suddenly you're near someone, enclosed in a circle with them, dancing, one stepping forward, the other back, one stepping back and the other stepping forward— perhaps twice. You may decide to step out of the circle. But you don't consciously step in."

She wondered how her mother fit into that circle, who had stepped forward, who had stepped back. "You make it sound so... random."

"I'm not positive it's random."

"There's a God?"

"There's at least a meant-to-be."

"Oh, please," Liza said, urgent, passionate. "Don't say that."

Honour was startled by his child.

"I was meant to be anorexic?" she asked. "Mom was meant to be an alcoholic? Or even, I was meant to be President or something. What good is that? What part do we play if things are meant to be?"

"I guess I was thinking of... people."

"Love?" she asked.

"Love, I guess."

Honour wondered if she would pursue that; Liza turned away from it.

"And what have you lived for?" she asked.

"Is the past tense necessary?" he said, smiling, reminded of how young she was. "My life isn't over."

"I thought I knew what you lived for. I thought I knew up until now but now I'm not sure. So the past tense."

"You don't want to hear about the present?"

Liza hesitated. "No."

She was staring at him now, tissues littering her lap, her eyes puffy and red but alert. He felt the pressure of her gaze on his face.

"It's so commonplace it's embarrassing," Honour said. "I'm not as unique as you think."

"Then?"

"You, of course. My job."

"You like being superintendent," she said.

"I do. Although— we all think we should have done more."

"Such as?"

"Run a larger district. An urban district. I think I would have done a good job— made a difference." It was, perhaps, his biggest frustration – feeling trapped in a cozy job.

"So why did you stay?"

"Not sure. Never the right opportunity. This was so good – I didn't want anything less than ideal."

"But this was less than ideal."

"But as close as I could come."

"But."

"But. There's always a but, I fear. If you're a thinking person." He tried to say the next part gently. Did she really need to know at sixteen that life wouldn't be ideal? "Nothing is perfect, you know."

She blinked as she took that in, like she'd swallowed a small pill and she was ready for another. "What else?"

"You won't believe this."

"Mom," Liza said.

"It's true."

"But you're... involved."

"It's over— Mom and I," he said. "You know that. You knew it."

"And the whole thing was a sham."

"No! It— should have worked. That's why it's so painful."

"Then why?"

"Don't ask me why," Honour said. "I don't know. There were too many *but*s in Mom's life. Too many, and she saw them all. Made others up."

"She envies me," Liza said. "My life. Wants to live my life."

"She envies us all, I'm afraid."

"I'd give it to her. I would."

* * *

Liza felt her toes the most. Balancing on the edge of the pool, arms bare and cold and tight behind her, she was anxious for the bell to go off, to burrow for a few moments beneath the water, to muffle the crash of diving bodies with a silence like space, an unnatural, surreal, blue silence.

Changing Color

I am sitting in the garden watching my tulips grow. There are ten tall stalks whose flat leaves turn a deeper green each day. I planted them two seasons ago then forgot them until the first leaves pressed through the icy mulch, poked through dried leaves and sticks and grew despite me. I discovered them splayed against the ground, draggled but alive.

Planting them was a small pleasure, then. I knelt on the damp earth, grass sticking to my bare feet, my swollen knees. Leaning over as best I could, my bulging stomach pushed warm against my thighs, I cradled each papery bulb in my hand before laying it carefully in the hole I had dug for them. I placed each one in the dirt, pointy side up. They looked like brown garlic, like lumpy onions. Then I gently pushed the earth over them, leaving them to winter. You kicked. I remember you kicked, right then.

Not all of them came up. Perhaps I crowded them in too small a garden; perhaps I knocked one on its side. But I root for them all; I try to take care of them all.

One is especially tall and strong, her leaves wider and greener than the others, her stem thick yet resilient. She was the first to lift her heavy leaves toward the sun, the first to bud. Though none of them have flowered, she is already the queen tulip, reigning at the center of her bowing ladies, feeding off their beauty and generosity. I am appalled by her, and enthralled.

I spend an inordinate amount of time sitting alone by my tulips. My neighbors are beginning to wonder. I start to bring out a chair with me, a book. I turn a page occasionally so they think I'm reading. But I cannot. I soak in the late spring sun; I take off my sandals and burrow my toes in the grass, in the dirt. I watch my tulips. I want to see them flower, to see their orange or red petals blossom. I want to witness their moment of grandeur, their triumphant debut.

* * *

"She's so beautiful," he said.

I held you in my arms. You were ugly and old-looking, wrinkled and supernaturally red. All tummy, you had skinny arms and legs, bent like a crab's, that wriggled around you. You smiled and stopped, smiled and stopped, your muscles not strong enough to form a grin. But your gaze was steady, tiny blue eyes that wouldn't let go. They squeezed my heart.

"Isn't she?" I said. I could barely breathe.

Elizabeth. A long name for such a small entity. We wrapped it around you like a blanket. We had planned on shortening it to something cute and modern – Bethie, Lizzie, Zee. But we never could. If anything, your name ended up longer. "Elizabethie", we said, tucking the extra syllable around you.

Your cries and whimpers and squeals filled up the house. Your slightest sound sent us running. Even when you were napping, we listened. On the monitor, your gurgles sounded alien, a radio broadcast of static-laced slurps, tiny sighs and delicate coughs. Sometimes you giggled in your sleep.

Sometimes you woke up screaming; there seemed to be no pause between sound sleep and pure terror.

* * *

"And what did our princess do today?" he asked. Still in his suit, he bent over your crib, catching his tie before it dangled in your face. You smiled for him, moved your arms about in a circle, as if you were swimming. You gurgled like a mourning dove. Performed. You were happier than you had been all day. "Eat a little? Nap a little? Poop a little?" he asked.

"Exercise her lungs," I said. "A lot."

"Oh, are you making sure your lungs are big and strong?" He smiled at you, nodded his head encouragingly. He seemed enormous next to you, as bulky and awkward as King Kong. "You make sure you do that during the day, for Mommy." He wagged a finger. "But not at night! There's more oxygen during the day."

"Gee, thanks," I said. I walked over and wrapped both my arms around one of his. It was meaty and muscular beneath his starched blue shirt. His free arm reached toward you. He placed his thick finger in your skinny, wriggling hand and you squeezed. I watched him watching you, watched him tickle your double chin with his thumb. "I wish you would tickle my chin," I whispered.

"Oh, does Mommy want her chin tickled?" he cooed in the same voice.

* * *

"She's a difficult one," the nurse said cheerily.

You were whimpering as I put you to my breast, as I put my

breast to you. You wanted no part of it, you thought. At a few hours old you already seemed to know what you wanted. I placed my nipple near your mouth but didn't put it in— I wanted you to come to me. For a moment I felt your tiny lip on my breast, wet and warm, and then you jerked your head away as if on purpose. More new cries. Everything a first.

The nurse stuck her raw, chafed finger between us, turned your head and pushed my breast so my nipple filled your mouth. I almost pulled it out – it looked like my breast could smother you. But then you sucked, so hard it hurt; I knew we'd done it right. "Can't be shy," the nurse said. I felt reprimanded.

Sometimes I still needed to force it into your mouth; you often fought the breast. I'd let you fuss first. Difficult. I wondered if you'd always be difficult. But then you'd suck, pain and relief at once. Who would think you could suck so hard, my nipple pulled long and taut, like the umbilical cord we had to cut.

* * *

You slept on your belly, your limbs curled in around you. So quiet, so peaceful. I was going to look only, watch only. But I didn't see your back trembling, your blanket shifting; I didn't see any sleepy spasms in your fingers. You weren't supposed to be on your stomach. Had you rolled over already? I leaned into your crib, trying to place my cheek near your lips, to feel your hot angel-breaths. I felt nothing. I leaned my large face closer: still nothing. I was about to panic when you sneezed, woke, cried. I patted your back to soothe you, but you wouldn't quiet down. You screamed. I picked you up. Aaron poked his head in the nursery, a towel hugging his waist.

"What did you wake her for?" he asked. "Why do you make it hard for yourself?"

* * *

My tulips are beginning to reveal the secret of their color. Their brilliance is peeping out beneath the enclosing bud, which for so long was dark and protective, sheltering their vibrancy and life.

In just a day they are fully in bloom. I marvel at the speed of their opening, the medley of color. Three tulips are deep fuchsia, gorgeous and sad as promise. Two are a tropical Miami orange, with a deep summer shine. Several are striped two colors – pink and white, yellow and orange.

Yet something about them looks weak-kneed and limp. At least compared with my centerpiece. Although plain yellow, she has the largest blossom, the sturdiest petals. If I had to name her I would choose Jane, or Sue. There is nothing elaborate about her, yet her fragile power affects me. Plain Jane. Sensible Sue.

Aaron walks by me as I sit in the grass. I listen to his heavy footsteps passing me, for the hundredth time, it seems. He's early, the first time he's home before dark in weeks. Or maybe the days are getting longer. The sun sends weak light in our direction.

"What are you doing?" he asks. We never ask "how" anymore, just "what".

"Nothing." I don't open my eyes, don't move.

"I bought some bread for dinner," he says. "And wine."

Though the sun is dipping dangerously close to the hills I feel warmth like candlelight. I remember the round of a wineglass cupped in one hand, his fingers cupped in my other, as we sit cramped in our small kitchen. But the light flickers. We haven't eaten dinner together in weeks.

I hear him clinking pots in the kitchen, setting the table for two. "Honey, come inside." He uses his authoritative voice, the one he must have been saving for you.

"I'm not hungry," I say.

"Keep me company," he says, changing tactics. I pretend not to hear him. "Hon. C'mon!"

I shake my head so slowly I can feel my muscles creak in my neck. When I open my eyes to peek at him he is gone.

* * *

I needed to put on your coat for a walk. You'd been crying and fussing and I decided we both needed air. Round and round the park we'd go, several sets of mother-and-carriage. Some talked to each other but I always said an overly polite hello so they wouldn't bother me. I had a disdain for stay-at-home moms, although I had become one myself.

You weren't in the mood for anything that day. You raised your eyebrows, puckering your forehead as I put on my sneakers. "You're going to get premature wrinkles," I told you. "You shouldn't have such an expressive face." You looked at me blankly then, wondrous, all creases suddenly disappearing, and I laughed. "Silly."

As I approached with your coat you scrunched up your nose and scowled. I gently took one of your arms and you squirmed. You let out quick breaths that I recognized as the prelude to a tantrum. You began screeching as I succeeded in getting arm number two into the lavender windbreaker. "Damnit!" I screamed, banging my palm on the counter next to you, startling you, for a moment, into silence.

You screamed even more loudly, started shrieking as my palm began to smart. I zipped your coat up to your chin, slowly, trying not to lose my temper. "Shit!" I hissed again, irrationality building within me then dipping back down. Then I watched you calmly. Your brow was doubly wrinkled; your nose twitched. "Why do I have to do all the bad things?" I asked. "Put on your coat. Change your diaper. You won't hate Mommy for it, will you?" You were hysterical now, your face purple-red. "Is that a yes or a no?" I asked, then answered for you. "Yes, Mommy, I won't hate you."

By the time he came home you had fussed, nursed, napped. It could take you an hour to wake up, groggy and grumpy as a forty-year-old. Then, for him, you were all grunts and grins.

"She's been crying all day again."

"You're kidding." He lifted you higher, bounced you until you seemed as light as a doll. "Are you giving Mommy trouble? Elizabethie? Or is Mommy pinching you again? You squealed and squeaked. Then his adult voice, mock-accusing. "Once she starts talking," he told me, "you're going to have to stop pinching."

* * *

I have decided to cut down my tulips. Beauty is worth nothing. Their sweet faces bob in the breeze, nodding, agreeing. I kneel on the grass with the scissors, grasp them in my hand. My knees graze the dirt of the garden. I will cut the healthiest flower first. The scissors squeak open. Their metal touches the thick stem of my yellow star.

I cannot cut. The scissors squeak open but I cannot move to sever the green stem. It is too strong. It holds too much life.

I think of the fresh milky-green sap, the life-blood, inside the stems. I put down the scissors. I fill up an old plastic garden pitcher and water them instead.

* * *

The house was silent and dark. We lay still as if the slightest noise would wake you, as if the monitor were reversed. You were in your room but we whispered like stowaways, not wanting to get caught. We were talking about you, of course. After crying all day, you had been sleeping an hour, and we hoped for several more.

Finally, we hushed, prepared for sleep ourselves. He patted my butt. His fingers grazed my bare thighs. I reached for him and we were suddenly alone. "You," he said. "I remember you." I don't know how long it lasted but soon I was bearing the weight of him. He had just maneuvered inside me when I heard you, waking. A complaining old invalid, you were insistent, persistent, your whine pathetic and helpless. It seemed like you knew what we were doing, and disapproved.

"Shit," I said. He laughed, was suddenly hysterically laughing, barely breathing as he rolled off me. "Shut up," I said, sitting on the edge of the bed, bare feet searching for slippers. His guffaws increased, but he eked out a few words.

"I can get her."

"I'm so freaking tired," I said.

* * *

I would sleep out here if I could. I would sleep in my bed of tulips like a girl lost in a fairy tale. But something prevents me; a nagging sense of appropriateness filters through my madness. So I wait shivering in the cool May night, damp with dew, until he has gone upstairs. I wander inside then, turn off the lights as if I'm going to bed, and stray through the darkened rooms as if my house were a museum. Except there are no pictures to look at, just blank walls subtly lit by the moon and the domes of street lamps, her apostles. I rest occasionally in a couch or chair, curl onto the floor by the chair where I rocked you, the wood hard against my bones. This way, I never experience the shock of waking up – the shock of memory after thinking everything is normal.

I am roused by a gentle shaking of my shoulder, a warm hand on my arm and on my hip. He leans down, whispers. "I'll carry you upstairs," he says.

I stiffen, jerk away. I lean sleepily on my arm. "No— don't. You'll drop me."

"Come upstairs," he says.

I shudder, suddenly cold. "I'm not tired," I say.

* * *

I was wearing a purple silk dress with a red sash, preparing for our first outing alone since we became a threesome – our (his and mine) anniversary. I click-clacked to the bright lights of the bathroom, make-up bag in hand. You were in your bouncy seat – bungee jumping, we called it. I strode past Aaron to the bedroom for my eyeliner, and noticed you watching me. I sidestepped in front of you; you followed me the only way you could – with your eyes. They shined light hazel, flecked with green some days, yellow others, so large they made you look skinny, though you were a bouncing cherub, in the 95th percentile. Your gaze fell about waist-level – my red sash.

I shuffled to the left; I shimmied to the right. Your eyes were wide and alert, as if you knew you would see only so much, as if you knew that you had to pay attention. I tap-danced in a wide circle around Aaron, my arms flailing back and forth like Gene Kelly's. Both pair of eyes, now, bright and adoring, followed me closely. You squealed with delight.

I scanned the baby-sitter for bloodshot eyes or burned-out hair or the faint afterwhiff of pot. But she seemed more efficient than I was, asking where the diapers were and the time of your last feeding, details I'd forgotten to tell her. Everything about her was tidy and calm: her pale folded hands, her tucked-in ironed t-shirt, flowers embroidered on her breast pocket.

We guiltily slunk out the door. I felt naked leaving you behind. At dinner, I fingered the red silk beneath my white, linen napkin. I was reluctant to hold his hand; it meant letting go of the sash. It meant letting go of you.

* * *

Black is fashionable anytime, necessary only sometimes. Convenient, actually. I had several dresses to choose from: long and flowered, long and plain, short and flowered, short and sexy. I fingered another dress, bright purple silk, red silk sash. Inappropriate but it's what I wanted to wear. Then I could know you'd be watching me.

I chose the long, plain dress instead, sober and fittingly tragic, then took the red sash and wrapped it around my neck. The end of it trailed down my back.

* * *

We were trying to get to sleep early – adult time for reading or renting a movie, another habit we seemed to be giving up. Instead, I listened to the silence. "Do you think we should check on her?" I asked.

"You'll wake her up."

Not a gurgle. Not a sigh.

"She's never this quiet."

"That's good, isn't it?" he asked, sensibly. He turned to hold me, to warm away my worries. He wrapped one hand under my breasts; he slipped the other beneath the elastic of my cotton underpants. The silence was drowned out by his hardening, the slow, increasing caresses of his hands then lips. We didn't get to sleep early, but, eventually, we slept, and peacefully.

* * *

He discovered you. "How's my princess today?" he sang as I filled the coffeepot with fresh water. "How's my sleepyhead?" He opened your shimmering, white blinds. I took the coffee out of the freezer, measured out the frozen grounds. "Elizabeth?" His tone was unusual. Something attracted my attention. I heard, "Elizabeth— Oh my God!"

I ran to your door but I felt like I was not moving at all, as if the room, your crib, the light from your window, were moving around me. He was holding you to his shoulder, patting your back, as if you needed burping, then rocking you with his arm. Your entire body fit into the crook of his elbow. I went to hold you, to take you, but something told me to think. "I'll call 911," I said, my voice sounding outside me. I found myself in the kitchen listening blankly to the dial tone. I didn't remember what to do. Then I hit three buttons, heard them say, "Mrs. Josephs?"

I was excessively polite. I said, Please and Thank-you. I said, Please come. My baby isn't breathing. Please hurry. Please.

He was kneeling on the floor then, curled over you, as if in an extravagant bow. "Let me see her," I said. I wanted to find a minor problem, a minor glitch. Like I could switch the batteries around; like I could fiddle with the plug. "Let me see her." Slowly he stood up, stretched out his arms, holding you, extending you to me like an offering.

I learned the meaning then of stone cold. I cradled you in my arms. I pushed you underneath my breasts. It was always warm there, even warmer since you came. I wanted to warm you; I wanted you to be warm. When the medics arrived I refused to give you up.

My eyes were dry until the night after the funeral. Wind pierced my eyes; no tears soothed them. I watched you, my still infant; nothing closed my eyes. Until we were trying to sleep and I could hear only silence.

After I was crying for ten minutes, after I began heaving and gasping, he held me. He placed his hand under my breast; he slipped a finger beneath my underpants. "Don't," he said. "I don't—" Don't think don't feel don't know what happened don't cry. By habit he grew hard, but we pretended not to notice. Don't. When I woke, I was lying at the very edge of the bed.

* * *

Overnight, Elizabeth, a transformation. I find my Yellow Sue, my Plain Jane, is changing into a tiger, a jungle lily. A Suzanna, a Janette. Black stripes now charge up her petals. I miss her simplicity, but I am in awe of her brilliant sophistication.

The next day she has changed again, her yellow deepening into a velvet orange, sweetened by a tinge of pink. Yesterday's brazenness turns into today's beautiful regret. She is my flower, after all.

* * *

I don't turn to look at him but I listen. Aaron's steps don't pause, though the sun is hours from its end; his steps scrape busily by me, thin dress soles whistling against the cement walk. The afternoon is extra quiet now; even the tulips have stopped their chatter. A breeze picks up for a moment and maybe that is why I don't hear him stepping off the porch. "How is my princess today?" he asks. I look up and he's standing with your quilt, rolled up and stashed under his arm, as if he's taking it a long way.

"Where are you going?" I ask.

"Picnic," he says, oblique. He loosens his arm, catches the quilt with both hands, and throws it into the wind. Its sturdy cotton takes up the sky for a moment, clouds become patches of yellow flowers and blue dogs, which land so softly on the grass the blades barely bend. It is the first time the quilt is used; you never graduated from your receiving blankets, soft as your skin.

He has my attention now. He steps quickly down our walk, turns the corner. I hear the car door open and shut, and see him return, three grocery bags dangling by his legs. He eases them onto the quilt, goes into the house and comes out with plates, silverware, wineglasses, corkscrew. He sits sideways on the quilt, pours two glasses of wine. "C'mon," he says. "Sit with me." He brings out cheese spread, crackers, tiny grapes the size of dewdrops, shrimp salad and bread.

I leave the comfort of the beach chair for the quilt, carefully cross my legs so I am Indian-style, back as straight as I can make it. I clasp the glass he offers.

"Look," I say. "She turned."

He gazes at the tulips curtsying at the border of the quilt.

"Is that the yellow one?" he asks.

I nod, as if we've been discussing the tulips all along, as if I knew he'd been watching them too.

"That's amazing," he says. "I didn't know they changed colors."

"Me neither," I say.

"You know," he says, "in the morning, they're closed up." He holds his glass up to the sun, cups the curve of it in his hand like a tulip. "Like you." Shadows flash through the golden wine.

"Am I going to change color?" I ask.

We sit on this patchwork of white and blue, green and yellow, linked by thread so thin it's invisible, laden with holes made by a prickling needle which stitches together as it pokes, opening circles then filling them.

"Three months," he says. "Three months today."

"Is that all?" I ask, after a moment.

The fresh light of spring is deepening to summer as I sit in my garden, not wanting to leave the sun, not wanting the sun to leave. These are the things I wanted to teach you: Tulips. Grass. Red. Yellow. The sun sets, the moon is full. I am here.

Before Letting Go

She doesn't know which aspect of the piece makes her want to become part of the space of the room – the midnight safety of the gathered sheet, pulled up at one corner to protect, to comfort, to block the light so white, to be sucked on around saliva-wet fingers, to hide; or the white light of the window, its escape. Or which – she should clarify – which compelled her the more strongly, because "both" was the answer. Oh the push and pull of desire, the give and tug, up and away, of the cloth slipping, sliding from the corners – then stopped. One hard surface against another, three corners jerking it tight. Escape. Remain. She can't quite put her finger on the pulse of it – can't quiet the impulse to become a shadow within the linen-cotton blackness, or to slip invisible into the light.

My mother smiled as I took her picture, easy, affectionate, natural, as if she wasn't posing. And then – Oh, you've taken it? I didn't realize – and of course the rest were forced, revealing slightly odd smiles and a gaze reversing back on itself, the rest were *photographs*. The first was my mother, watching me. Eleven months later and I did not know what she was watching, if she was capable of seeing, her eyes wild as my brother asserted his voice to tell her I was there –

blacker than brown eyes, dulled by – was it the drugs? pain? the stroke itself? Brief, this was, the only blessed thing about it, when the weeks before had stretched out long and supple across the small space of her illness and over us all in curves and valleys and rivulets, filling every moment, giving us time we never elsewhere possessed except maybe with her as children. After my visit then she'd written, teasing, of how bossy I'd been while nursing her to recovery (we'd hoped) – the new side of me she'd seen. And now, hours after I'd returned, it was me watching her, holding her hand, singing, no matter whether she could see or hear, softly in the night halfway between dusk and dawn.

It was just an ordinary room. Yet how the light played on its surfaces, as if the light had sponged white onto the walls, water-colored the palest blue-gray for the shadows which were somehow darkest where the light was brightest. And then the light became its own thing, the light and the shade and the blackness of the surface of the cloth, the hollows of its shapes, the furrows formed with a lifting of an arm, a gathering in the hand, a *quick* (before all is lost) clutching of fingers – and held.

In response to the work, "Dam", by the artist Janet Passehl.

Long Division

It feels like one long night, the days that have passed since we arrived at this house where we used to spend so much time it almost felt like ours, and this dawn, after which we will leave again. Luminescent she looked that first night in the pale glow from the window: my wife, fresh from our walk to watch the moon rise over the Thérain. Her idea of course. She was always full of ideas. Even in that dim light I could see the beauty mark on her cheek. It darkened when she exercised, or talked animatedly with friends, or even just worked hard at her desk. Or was agitated.

"I'm sorry," I said. But the moment had slipped away. So many do.

We'd been here only a few minutes when we decided to take a walk before the light disappeared altogether. We put on the wellies left by the English couple who owned the house, and headed across the field toward the woods and stream where once we had walked in a rainstorm in these same borrowed boots. We sloshed into the brook to the other side and meandered through the small village of Canny-sur-Thérain. The houses were lit orange from inside as if the French still used candles at night. An occasional phrase floated through the early spring air, *"Merveilleux!"*, *"Mon cher"* and then, as we passed the smell of cooking, *"Ce canard est très bon."* We laughed. "Why do I feel at home here?" Rae mused, and I reached for her hand, cool in the air of the approaching night. We have lived in Cardiff now for a decade, the University accommodating both my mathematics and her linguistics (*math with words*, she used to call it), but sometimes we still felt a separation between ourselves and that land, between ourselves and the voices, though we couldn't quantify it. We never felt the same distance here.

I was comforted too by the solidness of her short body as she walked beside me. She is slender but squared off somehow, like a long division symbol, her sparkiness in that initial, upward check that connects to the long bar over the dividend. I am tall and lanky like a quaver, and I worry sometimes that she can't reach me. That she stops before I begin.

We walked for a while, then circled back in the dark, later than we should have without a torch, though the moon was bright enough, casting shadows in our path – the bushes in the dirt road between the houses, the wall of the house of the *très bon* duck, the trees slanting tall and thin toward the stream as if directing our route. Our presence in this spot of the earth is so precise, so unlikely when measured against the vastness of possibilities of people and places on the globe: Rae and I at Canny-sur-Thérain. Latitude, 49.601 degrees North; longitude, 1.72 degrees East. Two of us on one pinpoint.

"How does this happen?" I asked, calculating the possibilities. "One with one. On one."

"Equals one," she said.

This was an old debate, she always sticking up for the idea of two merging into one couple (word singular); I, the mathematician, seeing two separate whole integers even when joined into one set.

"Equals two," I corrected her, easily, as I used to.

She stopped walking. "Equals three."

I said nothing.

"Sometimes," she added quietly.

The night became silent then, as if the owls, the wind, the Frenchmen in their glowing houses, were embarrassed by our argument. We resumed walking. Then, past the last house, "*Où est ma petite fille?*" *Where is my little girl?*

We arrived back and Rae stood inside in the moonlight taking off her scarf, her coat, her face turned away from me until I said I was sorry. She glared purposefully at the floor.

I had not wished to try. I had calculated the odds and for us in particular they were slim indeed. "I hate your numbers!" she'd cried out once. But I did not see how the hours of planning and minutes of effort could outweigh the heft of those figures, how the blossoming of hope would not drown us both as it turned into grief. I may have been wrong but my calculations were right. "Once," she had pleaded, "at least once," and it was here in the dusk of a warm summer day when we learned it hadn't worked; we had not been back since.

Are we not complete in ourselves? I wanted to ask. Each set is complete, each subset itself a set, complete on its own. Could we be made incomplete by something that does not yet, might not ever, exist?

She stood still and silent and firm.

"I know you're sorry," she finally said. "I know you're sorry we weren't able to – did not – have a child." She nodded vigorously as if convincing herself all over again. "But you're not sorry. About our decisions."

She took a breath and held it in – her body suspended in it. I was suspended in it, too. A window creaked. An owl hooted.

She waited for me to disagree. I did not. She breathed out. Switched on a lamp. Made tea.

Now after three days of walking around each other as well as the land I stand alone watching the sunrise.

So many moments lost. Even those lost in this house could barely be counted up, each four-day weekend containing so many of them. We'd been here maybe five or six weekends every year, and we've been coming here now for nine years, though we stayed only twice the first year we discovered the house, so that would be 5.1 with 1 as a repeating decimal weekends per year that we've been here. I multiply that by hours of daylight and a few moonlit hours when we've both been awake, and add the three weeklong holidays we'd had as well, which means if there were even one lost moment in each hour together that alone was one thousand seventy-one, point 9, repeating decimal, lost moments. Which is nothing compared to the moments lost in an entire lifetime, so numerous we couldn't possibly remember them all let alone realize they were beyond our reach. They were all lost, the moments; even those that had been grasped were gone now.

"Dah-vid." My name said the Welsh way.

Rae was standing at the doorway, her red robe flaring under her black hair, lengthening her petite figure.

"You're counting," she says.

I turn back toward the window to gaze at the weak rays of the sun rising over the Thérain. I cannot help but look at the sun directly although she always tells me not to. "There's so much to take away," I say.

Then she's in front of me, blocking the light, holding both my hands, her beauty mark milky black in the dawn. "Count for me," she says. And I do.

In response to two paintings by Tig Sutton: "Moonrise Over the Thérain Valley' and 'The Sun Rises Over the Thérain River".

Lips

His lips on her mouth, her breast, her stomach, her neck, her fingers – still after all these years she could feel them, tasting, probing, could recall them as if he had kissed her yesterday, uttering words that she could no longer recollect but hear only the sound of, their timbre, their rhythm, the sensation they caused within her – a reconfiguration of who she was.

Five months and five days they knew each other, lunching, coffeeing, wine-ing during all those hours Dominic was busy, dinner-ing when Dominic was artifying – this was Will's word for it – artifying in Italy or Spain or, for a month of their five months, the Dominican Republic. For the first time she had been invited but not welcomed. "What if you get bored?" he'd said, as if she'd ever gotten bored. And so she made a point of not getting bored in London, out at night, out during the day, stabs at art when half-drunk at midnight, the only time she dared to use the small room she didn't call her studio. Half-drunk at midnight was an excuse, too. Will told her that. Not that it prompted any sober mornings. And so she foreign film-ed and charity-shopped and café-ed more and more with Will. What had they talked about, what words had he said? Finally she kissed him. Found his lips in the half-dark of her kitchen late one night after cooking him dinner, licking crumbs of chocolate off his chin. Later, they recollected, a whole week later, they talked about their ancient history, their before and after: how he hadn't known what to do. Every time he looked at her she was staring at him. She blushed when he told her, hadn't realized. And yet he'd known that she wasn't free. He corrected himself. "That you aren't free." Why did those words stay with her when all the others wisped away? The "that", even.

And yet how insubstantial it had all seemed at the time compared with Dominic. He hadn't even noticed Will, hadn't really seen him, the latest twenty-something assistant in the gallery, though he tended to *see* the twenty-something women, including her, five years before, when she was just an art student and Dominic the latest *artist provocateur*. Fifteen years isn't that much older, she'd told her father, but in truth it was one of the pleasures of it, his stature; he'd given her weight, substance, a place in the world. Even Will's body was slighter, his shape like a girl's, long and willowy, his voice like wind chimes under Dominic's thunder. So she couldn't imagine him once Dominic arrived home, couldn't conjure Will up in her head even if she had just fucked him the night before. He, they, weren't a ghost of a thought.

And then there was that moment in the gallery when she promised herself she would tell him – just tell Dominic. She was in love with someone else. She was in love with herself in love with someone else. Tell him while Will was in the room, his hand on her arm, his lips under her fingers. She didn't reveal her plan; wanted him without any expectation or hope to hear the words escape her lips, clear, definite. She was free. *That* she was free. Will was showing her a new exhibition the day before the private view, the only perk of a gallery assistant, showing off his knowledge of the paintings, the artist – Will at his worst, in a way. She was sick of the art world, and still she was enamoured with his words, *blue-black*, *brushstrokes*, his low mutter in her ear. Intimate, as if he was saying he loved her.

Then Dominic phoned. She sees it now as if she is another person in the room, watching from the door, sees herself raise the phone to her ear, her fingers to his lips. But not to touch them. To quiet them. Still she can feel Will's unforgiving lips under her fingers. "Sssssh," she says. "It's him."

In response to the painting "Lips", by Harry Holland.

My Life in Dog Years

I quit my therapist last week. "I don't think anything is really wrong with me," I told him. "And I don't see the point in talking about fluff anymore."

I couldn't believe what he said.

"Well, I'm very disappointed." He had on his genuine voice – I'm listening, I care. "I was really getting a lot out of our sessions."

Quitting my therapist means I have an hour to myself today between filling Mike's blood pressure prescription at CVS and picking up Jessica from school. I'm tempted to get lunch at the new sushi bar in town, to admire the rolls sitting on a tidy wooden platform like girls sunning themselves on a deck. Instead I go home. Maybe I'll read that book I've been wanting to finish, maybe I'll just sit in the sun and do nothing.

As my key scrapes into the door, I can hear Chipper's nails click-click on the linoleum like tap shoes as he saunters over to greet me, pushing his nose against the crack. I open the door gently so I don't hit him, and he seems grateful, tail wagging lazily as he slicks his nose against my leg. "Chipper, stop it," I say, but I bend down to pet him, let him lick my chin as I rub his ears, feeling for the edges where the fur is soft and silky.

I love my husband and my kids more than I can describe, but God I love Chipper. He's always home waiting for me, happy to see me. And I know I do a good job with Chipper. I give him the kind of love he needs. Even with a dog, that feels like an accomplishment.

I poke around for that book until I spot the overflowing hamper, the ironing pile growing higher every time I look. The refrigerator needs cleaning and the light in the hallway is out. I put the dirty cereal bowls into the dishwasher and rearrange the dishes to fit in three more glasses. I forget all about doing nothing as I add detergent, then write out the phone bill. My therapist says I don't do enough for myself. Well, not to sound like my daughter Jessica, but— Duh? I do have a family to raise.

I decide to attack the ironing first, and once I start I don't really mind. I shimmy the board out of the closet, nearly bang my foot, but then it's up and the iron's heated and I put on an old plaid shirt of Mike's with the sleeves cut off so I won't get too hot. Jessica complains the loudest so I start with her clothes. At thirteen she already has good taste, though we can't afford good taste, and I admire the thick cottons as they send steam whooshing into the air, how they smooth out quick and clean, give off a scent like hot bread.

In truth, this is more soothing than sitting across from my therapist, trying to come up with things to talk about. I started seeing him when my mother died last year, not because I couldn't handle her death, but because I knew I could. I was afraid I would not mourn her enough, that I would bury my grief while it still needed to breathe. But we stopped talking about Mom months ago. Instead, we talked about drivel. I'd tell him that Jessica did badly on an exam and Mike was mad at his boss and Danny said something really clever the other day. Fluff, fluff, fluff, and then I'd leave. What was the point?

Mike says it's my part-time job at the veterinary clinic that's getting me down, but I like meeting all the animals. You can't tell too much about a dog or a cat in a few minutes. Like a person, you have to be around them for a while, and they don't always act themselves in stressful situations. But you can get a hint. I have favorites, ones that stick in my mind although they only come in once a year or so – the tabby who always looks angry in his too-small carrier, the Great Dane who tries to hide the limp he never lost after being hit by a car.

Though I have to admit it's more like a hospital than I expected. People tend not to bring in their animals for check-ups; they usually wait until they're sick. But I'm just the receptionist. I check them in. I check them out. Unless there's no pet to bring home because they're too sick, because they're being put to sleep. Then I have to give the owners a bill. Funny, but it's the only time people don't look at the amount. It's the only time I don't get any arguments.

Mike says I care too much about the animals, about the ones who die. But that only makes me want to do more. First I thought about being a veterinarian's assistant, and now I want it all— to become a veterinarian, to go into practice with Toby, the vet. But I haven't told my family this. What am I supposed to say? I'm taking college biology while Jessica takes it in high school? I'm going to grad school when she goes to college? We can't afford her tuition, let alone mine.

As I'm ironing Mike's shirts, I remember it's a half-day at school, and I'm late to pick up Jessica. She'll be mad – she needs to get to the orthodontist before going to her first day ever of cheerleading practice. I quickly grab Mike's lunch that he's left again on the counter and I wonder how I gave birth to a cheerleader. Tennis player, maybe. Flutist, more like it. Actress, possibly. But never a cheerleader.

Jessica. I named her after a high school friend, but as she gets to be a teenager she reminds me more of these miniature Barbie dolls I played with growing up – Dawns. The dolls were about six inches tall with petite faces, long lashes and elegant wardrobes – sparkling palazzo pants, sleeveless black evening gowns. They weren't cuddle dolls. They weren't talk-to dolls. They were dress up and send to make-believe-party dolls. The dolls talked among themselves, had grown-up fights about what to wear to a ball. But you didn't talk to them. And in her girlish thinness, in the way her hair swings straight and perfect at her chin, I see Jessica – my daughter – as one of those dolls. Because I don't know how to talk to Jessica either. I listen to her argue with her friends, hear them exchange giggling secrets. But I never know what to say to her.

So I guess I haven't told anybody about becoming a veterinarian mainly because I don't want to tell Jessica. I worry she could see me as a secretary, as an assistant, but not a veterinarian. Moms aren't veterinarians in her world, and she'd rather just have me be her Mom. Sometimes, it seems the older kids get, and the less they're at home, the more they need you. The less they want you around, the more they're angry when you're not there.

As I drive up, Jessica is talking to friends so she hasn't noticed the time. They're all wearing little round sunglasses like John Lennon's, though they don't know that. She gets in the car then stares at me, slides her glasses down her nose to look.

"Ma," she asks, "*what* are you wearing?"

I forgot to change out of Mike's old shirt. It's even uglier now that I look at it – it's not only faded, but got splotched with dark brown from some chemical when I wore it cleaning.

"It's my ironing shirt," I say.

"You know," she says, returning her glasses to their proper place on her nose, "maybe you should try wearing one of the shirts you ironed."

I'm so pissed off I can't think of anything to say. My mother used to inspect me as I went out the door for school, for a party. Is that what you're wearing? Do you think that shirt matches? And I wonder if an awareness of appearance, a bowing to custom, is a trait that skips a generation, like red hair and twins.

"How was school?" I ask.

"School sucked."

I'm just old enough to be offended by the word "sucked", but I'm more worried about her not liking school.

"How in particular did school suck today?" I ask.

"Abby is driving me nuts. After homeroom, she…" And she launches into the latest complaint about her best friend Abby. Abby has been snubbing Jessica recently for a new girl in school. When they both made the cheerleading squad I thought that would help, but apparently it hasn't.

"You know, you don't have to keep hanging around Abby," I say.

"Mom, don't be ridiculous."

"Abby isn't acting like a friend anymore." Jessica doesn't say anything but I catch her rolling her eyes. "Don't let her walk all over you." Still no comment. "She's being a bitch."

The word pops out before I can stop myself. She stares, surprised, curious, as if she actually heard me. Then she looks forward again and humphs. "You just don't like her," she says.

This makes me angrier than the crack about my shirt. I've tried to raise my daughter not to be like me. I want her to be aggressive about what she wants, to be assured. I want her to walk away from all the Abbys she'll meet in life. And she is unlike me in many ways. She goes for all sorts of positions – class secretary, cheerleader – that I wouldn't have dared consider. Yet somehow her desires are superficial, as if I have taught her to want, but not what to want. She wants all the things that will fail to make her happy – the right clothes, the right social circles. She wants from without, instead of from within.

Then I think, I don't fit into your ironed shirts. But it's too late for that.

* * *

When I get to the garage, his lunch in my hand, Mike's on the phone, a line of waiting customers in front of him, a disgruntled-looking mechanic behind. Mike's eyes widen in thanks, he nods furiously at me or at the customer on the phone, I can't tell. "Yes, I know that Ma'am, I'm trying to tell you that we looked at the radiator and it was fine." I linger for a bit, hoping for some acknowledgement that I have better things to do with my day than bring Mike his lunch.

As I get into the car, Mike comes running out, lunch bag in hand as if I were the one who'd forgotten it. I watch his lumbering gait, the silver already streaking his black hair. His name is embroidered onto his shirt like he's a boy scout, the letters bouncing as he runs. He's my high school sweetheart, the one I missed too much not to marry after college, the one I came home for, though I didn't want to come home. We talked about moving to Boston— but then his mother became sick, and Jessica was born, and now a day trip to Boston is a big deal.

"Hey, thanks," he says, giving me a tentative kiss, not wanting to rub the grease from his shirt onto mine. "How are you?"

I nod though I suddenly feel overwhelmed by it all – the kids too much, the house too much, our life never enough. "Can you phone the house at some point?" I ask, reminding him I'm at the vet's this afternoon. "Check on the kids?"

He nods as his name is called on the loudspeaker, smiles apologetically and hurries back to his desk, to his whiny mechanics and impatient customers. What would he want to be, if he could do it all over again? A service manager? I doubt it, and I wonder how we ended up here, middle-aged and not doing what we want.

Yet Mike doesn't seem to mind. He isn't hankering for yachting lessons or an MBA; he seems happy enough with me and the kids and a job that gives us what we need, if not everything we want. I feel selfish all of a sudden, like my dissatisfaction is a luxury, my desires an extravagant ruby pendant that I dare not wear for fear it won't sparkle as much as I had hoped.

A few months before my mother died, I dropped by her house to find her not kneeling in her garden, not on a step-stool repainting the bathroom, but sitting straight-backed at the kitchen table, all dressed up, pocketbook in her lap, the straps limp in her hand, as if she had forgotten what she was holding.

"Are you going out?" I asked.

"No." She stood up, looking around her, trying to press the wrinkles out of her skirt with her hand. I wished I could find something small for her to accomplish – a bulb that needs replacing in the chandelier, a crumb on the floor. But my mother's house was immaculate.

"What are you doing?" I asked.

"Oh, I guess going to the mall," she said, yet I could tell she didn't want to go to the mall.

"Your bow's crooked." I stood before her, retying the bow on her silk blouse, making her look the way my mother always looked. "Shall I come with you?" And I did, buying her a new blouse, on sale, so she wouldn't feel guilty.

She died in her sleep a few months later, discovered by a neighbor who knocked on her door because he hadn't seen her that morning, watering her flowers. Everyone consoled us, saying, That's the way to go, painlessly, after a full life. Yet I'll always wonder if she just stopped caring – if that morning she hadn't gotten up because she had nothing to get up for. I don't think I want to die in my sleep. I think I want to die knowing.

* * *

By this time, I'm late for Danny too, but he doesn't care. He and his friend Jake are the only kids left on the hill near their school, and they're drawing. What kind of eleven-year-olds draw? Yet they seem like regular eleven-year-olds as they chatter in the backseat about how many days are left in the school year (fifteen, I tell them) and they groan and thrash about until Danny figures out I counted the weekends and he realizes there's only eleven. One day's a field trip, I remind him, and we get it down to ten.

"Hey, Ma, can we go for ice cream?" he asks. They haven't had lunch yet, so I tell him we have to pick up Jessica.

"Can't she drive already?" he asks, annoyed, and the thought alarms me. Soon enough. Soon enough Jessica will drive and Danny won't get excited about an ice cream cone.

Our lives go by as fast as dog years – seven years pass, and it feels like one. So after dropping Jessica off at school, I stop when I see the line at the Dairy Queen isn't too long. I'm happy to have them in the backseat, licking their melting cones before the ice cream drips away, and I wish, as I drop them off at home, changing my shirt before I leave, that I'd gotten one for myself.

* * *

When I finally get into work, it's chaos. Two dogs are growling at each other in the waiting area, another is yelping in an examining room, and a cat got loose while someone was taking its X-ray. "Oh, thank God you're here," Nancy says when she sees me. She goes back to catch the cat as I persuade the owner of one of the growling dogs to take his pet outside for a bit. The phone rings as I sit at the desk and then the other line rings and I make appointments as I hear Toby, the vet, dealing with his patients – two cats in for a check-up. The examining rooms line up three in a row, divided by walls that look solid but don't reach the ceiling. There's a feeling of privacy but anyone in the office – in the waiting room, in the back – can hear everything going on inside. "Okay, who's coming out of the carrier first?" I hear Toby ask, the natural tone of his voice, his easy calm, comforting me the way it must comfort the animals. "Okay, Fred, you're first." Then to the owners, like an actor addressing the audience. "It's always the boys who go first. The girls are smarter – they know enough to hide."

Toby's the one I talk to about becoming a veterinarian – the one who suggested it, when it was just my private fantasy. We hash out all the details – what schools are good in

Connecticut, how to get scholarships, what prereqs I might need before going, what my family will think when I tell them. But the truth is I haven't done a thing. I talk to Toby like it's all getting done – transcripts, applications, GREs – yet I've done nothing but talk. At home, I haven't even done that.

After Mom died I found a box of mementos from my childhood stashed in the attic – my high school yearbook, a few school papers, school photos going all the way back to kindergarten. Underneath all this was a book I made in third grade, written on red and yellow construction paper folded in half and bound with yarn strung through punch holes. A magazine picture was glued onto the center of each page, with a sentence crayoned in purple underneath, written in my scrawl. The cover read: When I grow up I want to be a doctor.

I don't remember ever wanting to be a doctor, but here were all the reasons listed, page by page. I want to be a doctor because I like to help people. I want to be a doctor because I like science. I want to be a doctor because I want to find the cure for cancer. I don't remember making this book, I don't remember knowing what cancer was, I don't remember feeling like this girl felt, confident, brazen.

Do you ever wish you could go backward? Start again and see if you could do it better on the second run? That's how far back I want to go, to the moment in third grade when I thought I could be a doctor.

* * *

Just as it's quieting down, a man rushes in the door, half-carrying, half-dragging a German Shepherd. The whiff of vomit follows them in and I can see the man's covered in it – black-green liquid that looks like no vomit I've ever seen. "My dog started throwing up – I brought him down right away – I don't know what's the matter," he blurts out. The dog breaks loose from him and starts running around the waiting area. I call out to Toby as the dog vomits on the floor, thin black liquid seeping across the linoleum, the dog bumping into walls and chairs like he's blind, growling and snapping as vomit spills out of him.

Toby comes out of an examining room and I'm running ahead of him to grasp the dog. "What's his name?" I yell out. "Prince," the owner says, and, together with Toby, I grab the dog the way I've seen him do in the examining room, reaching for his collar from behind. I whisper, "Prince, It's okay, Prince," though it isn't okay, and I don't mean to lie to the dog. "Let's bring him in back," Toby says. Prince pukes again near the desk, black vomit spreading all over, the stench almost gagging me. I hear a woman leave with her kitten – "I'll come back tomorrow" – and we get Prince in back. Toby says, "You're a big guy, aren't you, but we're gonna put you on this table now," and we hoist him up together.

"I gotta pump his stomach," Toby says, his voice still calm but his words quick, clipped. "But he's gonna kill us if I don't give him an anaesthetic. I don't want to lose the time, but I can't muzzle him when he's throwing up." He thinks aloud as he goes about the room assembling what he needs and I wonder who he's explaining it all to – me, himself, or the dog. It's my job to hold Prince steady and I stand at the side of the table and lean my body along his back to keep him down, my elbows on either side of his neck as I rub him gently on the back of his head, between his ears. He's strong enough to shake me off but doesn't. I can feel his ribs yawning open beneath me then contracting to get out more poison, to squeeze it all out. The vomit splatters as it hits the floor, and

I wonder if he doesn't fight me because he knows the enemy isn't outside him, but within.

He tries to stand up and I loosen my grip, nodding Toby away, thinking the dog's body might best tell him how to fight it. I lean forward to watch Prince's face. His eyes are brilliant, clear and completely unfocused, as if he can't see at all. Then he looks at me with a flicker of curiosity – as if he's wondering, for a moment, about the person who is holding him, or hurting him, or whatever it is I'm doing. He yelps sharply, the way Chipper does when he wants my attention. Then he collapses.

Toby comes over with the needle in his hand— it's useless, and we both know it. Prince's eyes are wild as he coughs and pukes, weakly this time, and his body begins to shudder. I hold him as if I can stop the shaking but I can't. When he's still, we know he's dead.

I pet him a little more and we bring in the owner, a beefy guy who's eyes are tearing up, but we're used to that. "He looks like he got at some poison," Toby tells him. "I don't think he could have been helped." We leave the owner alone with Prince and Toby wipes his own forehead with the inside of his elbow, the only spot not covered in slime. "You're a mess," he says as he eyes me. "Feel free to take one of my extra shirts in there." Then he stands there like he's going to thank me but doesn't say anything, and I'm grateful, because it wouldn't make me feel better. I feel too sick about Prince.

In the sink area Toby uses to wash up before surgery, I slip off the drenched shirt and drop it into the garbage. Even if I got it clean I wouldn't want to wear it again and remind myself of the poor, sick dog. I wash my hands and arms and rinse the cool water over my face and neck. My bra feels sticky, and with a quick glance to the half-open door I slip it off and wipe my breasts with a wet paper towel before I pull one of Toby's shirts, a peach-colored polo, over my head. It's larger than Mike's would be on me, and his shirt doesn't smell like our family's clothing – its scent is woody, oaky. It smells good after the stink of the vomit. It clears my head.

"Nice fashion statement." Toby grins at me as he comes in to wash up, lifts his dirty shirt off and stands there rubbing his thick hands and arms under the water, slathering his burly stomach and chest with soap. "I can't believe how much that dog had in him. I've never seen anything like it. I mean it's like he ate a whole container's worth."

"What do you think happened?" I hear the phone ringing on the front desk, and I know I should go answer it.

"The guy pleaded ignorance. No idea where he could have gotten it. No asshole neighbors who didn't like Prince. Nothing."

"Do you believe him?"

"People are so stupid about animals, I just don't know." We stand there silent, and I can tell he's thinking of the animals he's helped, or tried to help, whose owners should have known better, who shouldn't have been in Toby's examining room in the first place. "By the way," he says, "you were great out there. I mean I'm really glad you were here."

I feel myself flush and I'm trying not to feel good but I do. Toby can do this to me. He could thank me for writing a message on a Post-It note and I'd feel good.

On my way to the desk I look in and spot Prince still on the back table – abandoned. I'm shocked, and Toby hears my little gasp. "I know," he says. "I don't know how he could leave him either."

The rest of the afternoon it bugs me. A dog like Prince deserves a better death than being wracked by rat poison, burned in a mass crematorium and thrown away. Pets deserve headstones, a marked grave, as much as humans do. Even the worst of them are flawless; they give us love unrestrained by selfishness, and we, selfishly, give only what we have time for. It's why I like the angry tabby, because she realizes her owner could do better, as if asking, What are you doing to me? Get me out of here! I think Prince had that fight in him too. He bounded out of his owner's arms, stumbled around the room like he could run from the trouble – or maybe he was running at it, biting and growling as if the poison was a beast he could scare off and be done with.

When it's time to leave I tell Toby I'm going to take Prince home. He just nods, then insists on carrying the dog to my station wagon and loading him into the back. We need to fold Prince's legs a little, which are getting stiff, and tilt his head at an awkward angle, to fit him in. The stench of his vomit, his death, lingers on the dog, maybe on us. Toby pets the top of Prince's head, strokes his nose. "You're going to want to take them all home," he says as the door nudges shut.

As I drive off with a dead dog, I wonder how on earth I'm going to explain this to my family. The dog's body shifts as I turn corners, bunching to the left, then to the right. Yet I'm glad I'm bringing Prince home. A person can become imprinted on an animal if she helps it when it's frightened, or lonely, or just young. Somehow, in the few minutes of his life that I knew him, I feel like Prince became imprinted on me, as if he were the one there when I was dying, instead of the opposite.

* * *

Everyone's in the kitchen when I come upstairs – Danny drawing at the kitchen table, Mike pouring a glass of soda, Jessica on the phone, Chipper by Danny's feet. Chipper looks sleepily up at me but I don't meet his eye – I'm worried about the remnants of rat poison. I don't want him to come over and lick me.

"I brought home a dog," I blurt out, then realize it's the wrong thing to say. Danny's eyes light up, Jessica tells her friend she needs to go, and Mike stops pouring his soda and looks at me, tired, his face saying, Honey, we don't need another dog.

"A puppy?" Jessica says. "Let's see!" She and Danny race for the door, fighting to get there first.

"No, wait! I'm sorry! That's not it." The two kids stop and stare at me, and I must sound strange, my voice hoarse and dry. "A dog died today at the vet. I brought him home. I'm going to bury him."

"Mom, dogs die all the time at the vet," says Jessica, my grown-up, my know-it-all.

They wait for me to explain, Danny and Jessica standing by the door, Mike with the fridge half-open. "He was poisoned," I said. "The owner didn't take him home. He was so sick."

"What's his name?" Danny asks.

We leave Chipper inside and go to look at Prince. He's lying awkwardly in the station wagon in a way a dog wouldn't – head too sideways, his body slanted toward one side, not curled up and symmetrical the way a dog would lie. But he's still beautiful with his rough brown-on-tan fur, the black around his eyes. "He smells," Danny says. We look at his muscles, strong and almost plump, his big, thick tail.

"Sweetheart," Mike says, "your heart is too soft," and he goes to get a shovel.

Danny follows him as Jessica and I wait by Prince. She stands there, hugging her arms like she's cold. Then she looks up at me, crying, her tiny nose bright red, her eyes puffy. "Oh, honey," I say. "I'm sorry."

She shakes her head. "It's okay," she says. "I'm glad you brought him home." And I wait, wondering what's wrong. "I just don't want Chipper to die," she says in a small voice.

At first I want to laugh – at the selfishness of teenagers, at her shaky little voice, at the fact that Chipper is nowhere near dead – and then I'm angry for all the same reasons, because my daughter can't see past herself. And then all I want to do is soothe her. I think – Chipper isn't going to die – but that isn't true, so instead I just hug her. I feel her silky hair against my cheek, under my hand as I stroke her hot face. Her body shudders under my arms as she lets loose one big, quiet cry. It's the way she always cried as a child, in spasms of tears and hiccups that sometimes made Mike and I laugh despite her. Today she allows herself only this one, then breathes in and sighs. She feels silly already. She's ready to separate from me, her clutched arms unclasping, her elbows hinting at my ribs for more room. So I release her, though I'm not ready yet to let her go.

Mike and Danny come out of the garage with at least a half-dozen shovels and rakes, and we choose a spot near a line of red maples at the very back of the yard. Mike starts at one end and Danny at the other, their shovels clinking as they hit rocks, the dirt swooshing off their shovel and landing with a small thump. Birds are twittering in the trees, preparing for nightfall. Mike grunts a little each time he rises with a load of dirt, and Danny unconsciously begins to imitate him, as if that's part of how you shovel. Though we will take up our rakes soon enough, help spread the earth over Prince's body once Mike brings him over, for now Jessica and I just watch the boys. She looks herself again, her gold hair blowing slightly in the breeze, and I'm amazed at my family, as we dig a grave for a dog we never knew, no one questioning me, no one thinking I'm crazy for bringing him home.

The God Who Was Himself Whispered In Her Ear

If she could lose herself in the story, Serena thought, she could get over their fraught morning. The audience in the airy, white lobby of the Wales Millennium Centre began to settle down as the storyteller walked onto the stage, crossed it once or twice, then stood, tall and still, his long blond hair in a 1970s ponytail, his face bright red as if he'd "caught the sun" (one of her favorite new phrases). This is so British! she thought. In an alternative kind of way, not in a way she could have ever imagined in the States. Her plan of steeping herself in Britishness to soothe the homesickness she always felt when she and Rich argued was beginning to work.

The audience fell silent – even the customers in the cafés, the people streaming past on their way to other events, seemed to quiet into a hush as the storyteller began.

"One day" – his chin jutting out as he spoke – "a fool found an ancient coin on the ground near a wishing well. Roman? the fool wondered, intrigued for a moment."

Rich shifted next to her as if already bored. "...no great find in this ancient land." Unless he was still angry? *Stop it!* She shut her eyes as she sometimes did when she was read to, trying to take in the story, the storyteller's voice, trying again to block out the sense of loneliness that had come over her that morning like nausea as she waited for Rich to return from the distant planet of his ex-wife, every other person she loved an ocean away. *Listen!* she whispered to herself.

"…no point selling the coin on eBay; he would use it to make a wish. But what should he wish for? He might have been a fool but he knew people less foolish than he had blown their wishes on silly, selfish, superficial desires – for money (which never brought happiness) or beautiful women (who didn't love them). And when he finally thought of his – to be a lucky man – he tossed the coin toward the wishing well. It arced into the air, and as it was falling as neatly as a rugby ball kicked by a Wales No.10, a magpie flew from nowhere, caught the coin in mid-air, and vanished again. Our friend didn't even have time to salute the lone bird and cancel out the destiny of sorrow that the single magpie had just delivered to him. 'Enough of this nonsense', the fool said to himself, and to anyone else who would listen. 'Wishing wells and magpies, my foot. I'm going to find God and find out why I'm so unlucky.' And so he left, walking over hill, down into the dale, across the M4, and into the forest…"

The small audience laughed. Serena was pleased that she, too, had gotten the British jokes – even the rugby reference, though there was no way anyone could live with Richie and not learn to love sports a little (well, except for you-know-who). She caressed his leg, stole a quick look to see how he was, her rather anglicized but still fellow American. Pubs, Welsh rugby, Indian food were what he liked about the UK; cathedrals, male voice choirs, storytellers were not. He smiled back vaguely.

Good enough, she thought. And as she listened, rapt, eyes open now, the storyteller began to take the shape of the characters in his fable: optimistic, like the fool, as he stepped lightly, springily, from one end of the stage to the other; his deep, reedy voice threatening, like the hungry wolf in the forest as he asked the fool to seek God's advice on where he might find more food. Upright and thin, the storyteller became the straggly tree that asked the man to find out why it could drink no water despite being planted by a clear, blue lake. With his thick, yellow locks, the man turned into the beautiful woman in the pretty red house and a green, green garden, who asked the fool to find out from God why she was still so unhappy. Finally, the storyteller became the God whom the fool found juggling apples in a tree, telling the man, as the apples went round and round, round and round, mesmerizing the audience with the hint of eternity, that luck was always there for the finding: go look for it.

"So the fool took God's advice," the storyteller said, "and turned around to set off for home. On his way, he passed the beautiful woman once again, who wanted to know how he had fared. 'Well,' the fool told her happily, 'God said that I simply need to go find my luck.' 'And did you ask him about me?' She spoke tentatively, not knowing if she wanted to hear what this God had to say. 'Oh yes,' the fool said, 'you are unhappy because you have no one to share your life with; beautiful things are always better shared.' 'Well, man,' she said, reaching her pale arm out to him, 'would you stay with me and share my house, my garden, my life?' The fool answered immediately. 'Oh no, I can't. I must go find my luck!' And off he went."

Serena stole a look at Rich. Was he listening? He clasped her hand and widened his eyes at her; he was enjoying it despite himself.

"And when the man reached the tree and related what God had said, the tree, too, asked about his case. 'Oh yes,' the man told him, 'God said that there is a treasure buried in the roots of your tree. You must find someone to dig up the treasure, and then your roots will be free to soak up water again.' 'Oh, man,' said the tree, 'would you be kind enough to dig up that treasure for me?' The fool responded immediately. 'Oh, no, I don't have time, I must go find my luck!'

And off he went, through the forest, where he again met the wolf, and he repeated his story. 'And what,' the wolf growled, 'did God say about me.' 'Ah, yes,' the man said. 'He said you must eat the first fool you see.' And so—" the storyteller stood motionless, for a moment, then his voice rang out like a laugh "— the wolf did."

As the audience clapped, Serena found herself close to tears. Was this her fate, too? Would Richie never see? Their argument, leading a train of other, similar arguments, came rushing back. Didn't he know he had to appreciate what life had thrown his way? But this was an old story for her and Rich, too. She turned away so he wouldn't detect her tears.

* * *

Rich watched with part affection, part annoyance, as Serena went up to talk to the storyteller. He liked her American habit of having to meet everybody, talk to everybody, tell everybody how good they were. He still found it refreshing, as if his twenty years in the UK had made him one of them; it wasn't something Beth would have ever done. Would ever do, he corrected himself. She wasn't dead. Sometimes, though, he wished Serena could make a quicker exit.

The Millennium Centre was crowded on this Saturday

afternoon in April; people rushed to the Bay on these rare sunny days, families mostly, or couples on their own, streaming through the arts centre as if was part of a tour. He liked the inside of the building better than the hulking outside (it looks like Darth Vader, Serena always said): the way the stairs angled up two stories past the balconies, how the words cut into the steel façade became, from within, just geometric patterns like the stairs and the balconies. It couldn't have been an easy place to perform – perhaps the storyteller's presence of mind was as impressive as his story. The space echoed like a playground: the screeching children, the chattering parents, the chairs like park benches, the cafés, the ice cream truck, the banisters, the slides. He felt a pang: how he missed his daughters, his family, the Saturday afternoons when he and the girls and maybe Beth, if she were feeling well, would have ended up here, too.

Serena was still standing happily at the back of the queue of people waiting to speak to the storyteller; she had let a few people go ahead of her, so she wouldn't feel rushed. Rich wished suddenly he had gone up with her, was holding her hand; for as she reached the man and leaned forward to speak, her flaming red hair flashing over her shoulder, the storyteller stood taller and looked around him with a ridiculous, twinkly smile as if wondering if anyone else was noticing his surprising stroke of luck. Amid the couples walking past hand in hand, children skipping ahead of their parents, Serena and the storyteller stood in their own bubble, their bodies dipping toward and away from one another, exchanging business cards, cash and a CD.

Then Serena was standing in front of Rich as if she had been spirited there from the future. He kissed her quickly, hoping the other man would see; she was all atwitter. "He lives in Canton!" she said excitedly. "I've invited him to dinner!"

They left the Centre to take the walk they had planned, passing the petite black-roofed Norwegian Church ("it's so *cute*," Serena said) then reaching the barrage that stretched over the Bay to Penarth, where they'd stop for lunch. This walk was the main reason he'd agreed to hear the storyteller, though it would have seemed churlish not to after their argument, after she'd said how homesick she'd felt. Beth had asked him to come to the house to watch the girls for just half an hour, Serena telling him, quietly, She. Can. Bring. Them. Here. Crying when he'd said he'd be right back, that it made more sense to go there. And it had. Serena seemed better now, the storyteller, the walk over the Bay, doing the trick. "Maybe we could take the girls to see him," she said, her head bopping up and down beside him as she walked with her little bounce, "he says he does children's events, do you think they'd like this walk, though it's too long, maybe we could take the ferry over and walk from the Penarth side, they'd love that!" A little girl ran by with her nose dripping in the chill air, but with Serena buoyant next to him, his thought – he'd wipe his own girls' runny noses with his bare hand – lost its sting.

This was how he needed her to be – his beacon through all the darkness. "Shine bright," he wanted to tell her. "Keep shining bright." Instead he pulled her to the side of the bridge and kissed her. "You're gorgeous – do you know that?" She kissed him back through her smile, her eyes wet from cold or tears or maybe both, her breast pushed against his chest. He adored her. Her cold soft cheek against his, her girlish excitement about the storyteller, even her emphatic tears this morning as he left the house because he couldn't wait to get back to her; he was bound to help Beth first but he couldn't wait to escape to Serena. "What the hell are we doing on a bridge?" he grumbled into her ear. So they went home, to bed, Serena pointing out in the car, "God *did* say to find our own luck," and then at home, pulling off his jeans, "we are lucky, lucky, lucky," kissing his stomach, wrapping her legs around his waist, "lucky, lucky," until she couldn't speak for moaning.

* * *

Months later, Serena settled into a couch in the storyteller's house but did not look at him as he talked and talked, as her new friend tended to do, the new friend whom she had somewhat purposefully chosen to make plans with for the evening – the evening Rich was having dinner with his daughters at his ex-wife's house without her. Serena would never be invited to celebrate the girls' graduation from nursery school, or to celebrate anything else. Ever. Rich went anyway. Distraction, she needed distraction, she couldn't possibly sit home and stew over Rich's cozy family dinner, and she knew the storyteller, raconteur that he was over coffee, at her and Rich's house, and now at his own home, would distract her. He had the knack of seeming as if he was paying attention just to her, or whoever else he was talking to – though Rich thought it was just Serena. The storyteller couldn't take his eyes off her. So Rich said. He didn't much approve of her friendship with the man, but tonight Rich couldn't exactly complain.

Now, at the storyteller's house, she was stewing nonetheless. Did children really graduate from nursery school? It sounded like a lovey-dovey aren't-our-children-wonderful fabrication concocted by Beth to pull Rich back into her web. It sounded American, even, as if she'd begun using tools from her enemy's arsenal. *We can celebrate with the girls ourselves!* Serena had said, *And we will!* Rich had said. But the real celebration, the one that counted, Serena knew, was tonight; theirs would be a weak afterthought. Enough, enough. She remembered the storyteller used to be a clown. Maybe he could perform some slapstick for her: pretend to bump his head on the door, trip over the step into the kitchen. He had performed for twenty years with his wife, he'd told her a few weeks ago, until she moved out. He didn't seem haunted by her, though hints of his past, his own sadness, snuck out now and then – in some ways it was why she liked him.

She dared to look at him – she'd been avoiding his gaze all evening – and his blue eyes, startling in color, but also startling in expression, as if they'd just seen something absolutely amazing, were watching her as if waiting. He stood up quickly and stepped toward her then away then went over and picked up an apple from the cluttered coffee table, as if he might juggle just one, then sat down again. Books, a small flash light, a tea cup, a pair of castanets, were strewn across the table like an unruly still life; she wondered if he gathered them for inspiration.

"Your stories were great the other night," she said. "I wish the girls could have come." Beth had switched nights on Rich at the last minute (more bullshit). She tried to mention Rich and the girls when she could with the storyteller, when naturally she might. It seemed necessary. "Rich didn't have the girls after all."

"That's a shame. Though another venue would be better for them."

She nodded. He had told the story again of the unlucky fool, but this time she was listening alone in a small café, Rich staying home to watch a football match instead. "You didn't juggle," she said.

He laughed. "Forgot the balls. I added the juggling right before I told it at the Millennium Centre. I don't know if you noticed but a few people laughed at that part of the story—friends. Because I used to end my act that way, juggling. So I had made myself God."

"The story makes me tearful," she admitted.

"Oh, why?" He asked it casually, off-hand, as if this were still a light conversation.

Here was territory she hadn't entered with the storyteller; confessing her problems with Rich seemed another kind of invitation which she didn't want to extend. Yet did. "Well, you know. It's people not seeing what's in front of them. The treasures in front of them."

"Ah," he said. "*Carpe Diem*." The storyteller looked strangely at her, then down at the apple in his hand.

"What is it?" she asked. "I've made you sad again." Was he thinking of his ex-wife? Serena always worried that she dragged his grief out of him as if he were Rich; out, out, damn spot, out. She didn't want to make the storyteller sad just because she was – but what was it then? "I can't read your face."

He shook his head. "I don't know why you'd say that."

And she thought for a moment that he didn't agree with her interpretation of his tale – isn't it obvious? she almost said – then realized he didn't understand what she'd said about the sadness in his face.

* * *

Rich left his old house – his ex-wife's house – and headed home. Not his new home – he imagined telling Serena – just home. He wanted her to know it was how he thought of it in his head. He would tell her that, he thought, unlocking his door, calling out into the seemingly empty house. "Serena? Sweetie?" He would tell her that was what he thought on his way back from Beth's, give her that small gift in exchange, as recompense, for what he suddenly could see might have been a difficult night. "Serena?" But she wasn't home. The house seemed especially vacant, though it always did after leaving the girls. He packed away all the girls' toys to send back to Beth, although Serena didn't understand why some toys couldn't live here. His insistence that it was neater always seemed foolish after leaving the haphazard mess of girly objects in Beth's house.

She must still be with the storyteller. He'd been dying to come home to her; feel her body; remind himself why he had done all this. He wondered if he should worry.

Then the phone rang out. His heart lifted and he went over to pick it up. "Hi Sweetie," he answered to deep silence.

"Uh, Beth, actually," his ex-wife said.

She'd called because she had forgotten to discuss arrangements for the weekend, though really the plans were the same as always. He'd pick the girls up around six, giving Beth an hour to spend with them after work; he wasn't sure what variation she needed to discuss. *She does this on purpose*, he could hear Serena say, *so she can call you again, here*. But it wasn't true, he knew Beth, she was just forgetful, he wouldn't admit even the slightest possibility of manipulation on her part, even if Serena wasn't the only friend who'd called Beth manipulative, even if for half a second after each extra phone call he suspected Serena might be right, but they were wrong, they didn't know her.

He and Beth confirmed their weekend plans and she thanked him for coming over for dinner. "The girls loved it," she said and he flushed with pride. *This is why*, he would tell Serena, *This is why*.

"So that's what you call her then?" Beth said. "Sweetie?"

Rich stood still. What was he supposed to say? Yes?

"I mean, I'm so glad you came over, it was so good for the girls, but this is so—" she began to break down, the tears coming fast now, "so hard for me. I can't believe how hard it still is, I still don't understand, why, why did you do this, how could you do this *to them*, why..."

"Beth, please," he said. He let her cry at him for twenty, forty, he'd lost track, maybe sixty minutes. *Hang up*, he heard Serena say. Thank God she wasn't here.

* * *

"Can I try your piano?" Serena asked the storyteller.

So many books and CDs and magazines and even a bright orange wig perhaps from his days as a clown, or his ex-wife's, were piled on top of the keyboard cover that Serena wondered about the symbolism of these obstacles – he had clearly not been the piano player in the house. She was about to tell him not to bother when he began moving the items away.

"I'd be honored," he said, and he whisked them onto the coffee table, the window sill.

"Are you going to juggle all this?"

He obligingly tossed one light book in the air and looked pleased to catch it on his head. She laughed so he threw another backward, bouncing it off his heel. And then the piano was clear. She lifted the lid to reveal the ivory keys. "Now you're entertaining me," he said.

"Oh, I'm not very good," but she tinkled a few notes while she leafed through his music. Not too out of tune; maybe he did play. "Will you juggle to Ragtime?"

He shook his head. "Play something serious," and he leaned against the window sill.

She looked back at him and stood to shuffle through his

partner's Chopin, Mozart, Beethoven, then she put it all away and sat down again. "This is my homesickness singing," and she played Shenandoah. "Oh Shenandoah, I long to see you," half singing, half humming the words, "mmm, hmm, mmm, you rolling river," thinking of home, of Richie, of the blackness in his eyes when he missed his girls, of the emptiness in her when he wasn't there, "hmm-hmm-hmm, I'm bound away," her voice low, and the storyteller humming a harmony above her, their voices mingling. He stepped closer and stood beside her near the bench, his hand near her shoulder. The God in his story whispered in her ear: *Carpe Diem*.

She stopped, her head down.

"Serena."

She felt him breathing next to her, waiting. The sound of the silent piano filled the room. He could touch her now, he could kiss her. Would that help?

"You know your story?" she asked. "About the unlucky man?"

"Yes?"

"I always think it's Richie being the fool, not appreciating his life. Not appreciating me." She looked up, tears wet on her face. "What if I'm the fool?"

"Ah," he said, and stepped away. She turned back to the piano and clinked on a few keys. She wondered what he would do now, from the distance she hadn't meant to create.

"Play it again," he said. "I'll juggle to this."

And he stepped across the room gathering the apple, a ceramic pear that he'd said his sister-in-law had made, an orange. "This song's too slow!" Serena protested but she heard her own voice, lighter, laughing, and the notes from the piano flew off her fingers fast and jolly. He turned to stand before her juggling the three objects, apple, orange and pear going round and round, round and round.

Other Women

May wanted to walk into the home of her friends as if everything were normal. So she greeted them as always: she hugged first Jean, then her husband, Mark, receiving a kiss on the cheek from both of them. Jean's kiss was quick and effusive, given along with a stream of endearments and exclamations. Mark's had become tender lately, almost shy. When May first started coming to their home, when she first began rekindling her high school friendship with Jeannie, Mark had enveloped her in a rough, brotherly bearhug. Now that he was May's lover, he hugged her delicately. His hand lightly touched her waist-length hair, his lips barely grazed her skin, which was flushed a pale pink. Yet May and Mark never missed each other's cheek or turned their head to the wrong side. Their embrace may have been brief but it was graceful. For that moment, they were alone.

Today, this ritual was completed more swiftly than usual. No sooner had May arrived than the next guests were coming up the stone steps to their spawling, contemporary house, sets of four trotting legs, four waving arms, and two chattering heads. May would be the only guest with just two legs, two arms and one head. Although Jean had urged her to bring a friend, May simply could not anymore, not with Mark so near. She regretted now confiding in Jean the trials of being a single woman – the comically horrifying blind dates, the compulsion to keep trying, keep looking. Jean had become overly concerned about May's singleness, and May couldn't relieve her worries with the news that she had found someone, however imperfectly.

Jean was in her element: she flitted from one cluster of friends to the next, her short, blond hair bobbing as she spoke, her thin, muscular arms occasionally reaching out to emphasize a point or simply make a connection. Her face, angular with large, lively eyes, switched quickly from one expression to another: from eyebrow-arched surprise, to a lopsided grimace, to a frozen gaze of mock indignation, given away by the softness of her dimpled chin. Then her laugh, Jean's curious laugh, floated above the party in a spurt of glee – a series of high-pitched eighth notes rushed together, halting only for her to add a few quick words or to take a frantic breath, then tumbling on. Even after all these years, Jean's laugh still left May astonished. Yet it was so sudden, so rapid, so filled with uncontrollable gusto that one had to join in.

In this initial hour, Jean concentrated less on her fellow teachers from Ogden High School and more on their spouses or partners, then she spotted May, and immediately drew her over to the crowd. "Dave, Becky, you remember May, don't you? The reporter?" They nodded and said hello and May nodded and said hello back. "I think Dave and Becky are the only married couple still standing together," Jean added.

"Someone has to watch this guy," Becky said.

"That's your job," Dave said jovially.

Jean was enveloped by the next group and then May exchanged niceties with the couple, a bit mechanically. She was already tired of niceties. May just wanted to be around people she knew, and the longer she had known them, the better. This was probably why she had come to Jean a year ago to begin with. Ostensibly, an article in the local newspaper about Jean being named Ogden's teacher of the year had prompted May to phone; but it was more May's knowledge that when she called for the first time in almost ten years, Jean would recognize her voice.

Mark was certainly not what she had expected. May had been looking to rediscover her childhood camaraderie with Jean: their days as children swimming in the lake near their homes, playing gin rummy when it rained, gossiping, as they grew older, about Jean's boyfriends. And at first, that's what she found. Last Labor Day weekend, a few weeks after May had first called, Jean and May spent hours sunning themselves on the deck. They took turns smearing lotion on each other's backs and arms and legs, they reveled in the stifling heat they knew would soon be gone. Mark did most of the cooking that weekend, using the grill and emptying out Jean's voluptuous vegetable garden. May stayed over one night in one of the several spare bedrooms that had never been turned into nurseries. The next morning, the smell of bacon cooking downstairs and the sound of muted voices comforted May out of sleep.

But she also found Mark: steady, thoughtful, decent Mark. His round face was pinched and squished until he would have been homely if it weren't for something rugged about him. He was too honest not to be tormented by their affair, yet he was also considerate enough not to show it. He was different from other men May had dated. Usually, in the end, it seemed that May's relationships had been about the men – their sexuality, their insecurity, their mid-life crisis, their love. With Mark, May felt more integral. Mark wasn't having an affair with her because he needed to have an affair. He was sleeping with her because May had entered his home. Because May had walked in their door and he couldn't ignore her.

Becky was chattering about a new French restaurant in Old Saybrook called Bernard's, which May had heard about but hadn't bothered to try.

"St. Bernard's." Dave interrupted his wife. "That's what I call it."

"Dave doesn't like it, but really, just because the portions aren't large enough for five people—"

"You know how a lot of restaurants bring over little relish trays, or baskets of bread?" Dave paused, nodding his head. "Dog food."

"Dave, that is disgusting!" Jean, holding three used wine glasses, paused as she walked by. "There's no disgusting chit-chat allowed at my parties. Even outside."

"Jean," Becky said, "May hasn't been to Bernard's yet."

"Oh, May's never been into trends." Jean's voice trailed after her as she headed toward the kitchen. "May's anti-trend."

"Anti-trend's in," Mark said, taking Jean's place, in a kind of cocktail dance. He let his arm graze May's elbow; May felt the pain of his absence from her hand and waist and neck.

"Are you accusing me of being trendy?" she asked, eyeing him through the veil of her hair as it draped across half her face. She hid behind it as long as she could then flicked it behind her.

"By being anti-trendy," Mark said. "You can't win."

"As long as you're not conventional," Dave added, winking at Mark. "You'll have to be careful."

"No *Mad Men*," Mark said. "No Stieg Larsson."

"No Prius," Dave added, raising his eyebrows at May admonishingly. "And no marriage. Strictly prohibited."

"No affairs either." Becky spoke up. She grinned wickedly. "They say that's the most conventional rebellion of all."

For a few long moments, there was nothing anyone could say. May could hear two guys behind her talking about the stock market. "Not that I would know," Becky added defiantly.

"Well, I'm glad to hear that, dear," Dave said, guffawing quickly as Becky walked away. He turned to Mark as if May wasn't there. "Always the ice breaker. I mean, ice maker."

May sensed that she had become something of a curiosity at Jean's parties, at least among the men. She wondered now if she seemed a threat to the women. It wasn't that May was any more attractive than the wives, but she might make a fanciful contrast. Her mauvish-purple flowered skirt, a long flowing gauze, paled against the crisp cottons the wives were wearing. She drove a beat-up Honda, lived in an apartment in New Haven, where the crime and poverty, while only a half-hour from their rural suburb, seemed to them intolerable. They wondered about the never-seen-twice dates she had brought to other parties; they wondered if she had sex. And while the wives accepted May's fate as a matter of luck – or perhaps faulty strategy – May felt that their husbands wondered how a woman like her could be alone.

That was a riddle May herself never tried to solve. She had come close to marrying only once, when she was twenty-four, the same year Jean was married. How was she to know then what she wanted? For a year, Tim asked her, obliquely at first, then openly, but never formally with a ring after dinner at a fancy restaurant, when May might have been wooed, or embarrassed, into saying yes. He asked only offhandedly, as they were making his bed or riding bicycles or grocery shopping, which made his request seem tentative at best. Her

"I don't know" turned to "Probably" after a while, but never progressed any further. Tim, not uncruelly, gave her a nickname toward the end. "May-be," he called her. "Maybe Sullivan." He left her shortly afterward, and May went on with her life, never knowing whether she had made the right decision, or whether she had made a decision at all.

In the fifteen years since then, May had lost count of the men she had slept with, or, rather, had stopped counting. She didn't want to remember either the sum or its parts. She didn't want the mass of them growing larger with each tryst, clouding each new encounter, waiting menacingly to add one more to their ranks.

When she was with Mark, they evaporated. She forgot they ever existed. He became her only-ever lover. It was how she had hoped – had known – it would be when things were right. All her mistakes were forgotten painlessly, in one stroke of luck or genius. She didn't want to marry Mark, to watch the remains of his marriage splatter over them. She didn't even want to think about a future. She just wanted this interlude to last – separate, untouched.

Of course with Mark, she sometimes had a different power to contend with, one she had no control over, which visited her only when Mark was there. Light and lithe, it floated around the room, curling and curving near their feet, above their heads. Its whitish wisp echoed the shape of their bodies – the concave of Mark's back, the erratic triangle of May's bent legs. When they slept it slept, cozying against Mark's back, his body turned toward May. It was Mark, May decided, who made it come and go. She wanted to ask him to send it away, but May feared that if she acknowledged it, it would stay with them forever.

May met Jean again in the kitchen, as May was helping

herself to more wine and Jean was checking on dinner. "Heard you got caught in a marital squabble," Jean half-whispered as she washed out a few dirty glasses.

May could smell the potted herbs in Jean's kitchen window as she moved closer to her. "Is that what it was?"

"Becky thinks Dave's having an affair."

"Is he?" May asked.

"Probably," Jean said matter-of-factly. "He's done it before."

If before May had been taking Dave's side, she now felt her allegiance shift. "Jerk," May said harshly, then shook her head. She thought, You hypocrite.

Jean gazed at her strangely, four refilled drink glasses in her arms. "Such an innocent," she said, then left.

May wandered outside and, perhaps out of some odd sense of apology, joined Dave again, who was talking to another husband whose name she could never remember. May strained to hear Mark's voice amid the harsh rhythm of the partiers, their words sharp and staccato. Mark was trapped in a conversation about Ogden, where he was public works director. He was responsibly explaining why the town needed a water treatment plant and why sewer fees had gone up. Patient, steady, Mark's voice grazed by May, then hid again in the din of mundane chatter, then found her, circled her, wrapped her in warmth. "I've been trying to tell the Ogden water story for a year now," Mark said, and he repeated it once more. He made it sound like a fairy tale.

* * *

Soon Jean was announcing dinner with the flair of a medieval herald, ushering everybody in the door then somehow beating them to the table, pointing out seats. "Mark, sit at this end. Becky, here, next to me. Joe, sit next to Sandy— do you need something to drink? Mark, could you…" Without seeming manipulative, Jean soon had everyone arranged to her liking, in boy-girl order, except for Becky, who sat on Jean's right. The symmetry was broken by May's presence, but Jean didn't make that evident. Instead, she sat May between two men, including the only person May knew well besides Jean herself – Mark.

May felt oddly displaced. Usually, she would be helping Jean serve dinner, making sure there were enough utensils to go around, that the butter was out, that everyone had wine. Instead, not wanting to be presumptuous, May looked on helplessly as Jean buzzed around before sitting down. May missed the familiarity of Jean's everyday dishes, chipped and cracked from daily life. She took solace in the red plastic ladle Jean had brought out for the sauce. Faded and slightly bent from being left too close to a burner, it made May feel more at home.

May had dropped into their lives as suddenly as a child, but with less disruption, at least at first. She loved getting a sense of a family's rhythm, their day-to-day routine. She liked knowing Jean and Mark always had spaghetti on Monday, that Jean's habit of leaving her shoes wherever she happened to take them off – at the front door, under the kitchen table – annoyed Mark. As she learned these habits, May felt she, too, belonged. She began dropping by uninvited, and was always greeted warmly; if she never noticed any hesitance on their part, it was because there was none.

For the first several months, May avoided being alone with Mark, almost without realizing it. She would go with Jean on a quick errand rather than stay at the house. She got off the phone quickly if Jean wasn't at home. Once, when she saw only Mark's car in the driveway, she backed quietly out before she could be seen.

Yet it was impossible for May to skirt Mark completely. She finally bumped into him when she was at the State Capitol in Hartford looking into a story and he was attending a meeting. Naturally they went to lunch; it would have been rude, really, for one of them not to suggest it, for the other one to refuse. Mark proposed skipping the crowded legislative cafeteria. They went instead to a small, Italian place nearby, which was really just as busy, but with people they didn't know.

May wasn't used to seeing Mark dressed for business. His white shirt sat squarely on his shoulders, which were wide and thin and a little crooked, his left shoulder slumping slightly lower than his right. His face, a faded burnt-red, as if he were out in the sun or on a fishing boat every day instead of inside a musty office, seemed a little less haggard than usual and more placid.

They talked about the article May was writing, discussed Mark's town projects. May understood the mechanics of Mark's job, having covered enough small towns in her early days to understand sewers and bonding; Mark chuckled at the documents May was using to hunt down information.

"So you don't hate reporters?" May asked. She imagined Mark would be a reporter's dream – helpful, smart, patient about explaining technical details. She liked the idea of dropping into his office, watching his surprised smile when he saw her.

"Not at all," Mark said.

"You don't throw them out of your office when they come in asking stupid questions?" she asked.

"Never. They liven up my day."

"Oh?"

"Pretending to be interested in catch basins and RFPs," he said.

"Fascinating stuff," she said, smiling.

"Now if you walked in my office," Mark said, "it would make my week."

May took in the implication, tried to deflect it. "Unless I was Joe Citizen coming in to complain."

"Even then," he said, quiet, insisting.

"Are we all done here?" The waiter appeared suddenly. May nodded, looking down as if she could hide behind her hair, although it was pulled back into a twist for work. "Coffee?" the waiter asked.

"Please," Mark said. "Two."

Cleared of their dishes, the table left little for them to fiddle with. They both watched Mark fingering the curved, metal edge of the table. The waiter returned with the coffee and check, which Mark picked up immediately, waving away May's silent protest. The two of them added sugar but no milk to their coffee.

"Do you ever wear your hair down?" Mark asked, tentatively, not looking up.

"Sure," May said.

"Maybe you could, sometime." Mark kept stirring his coffee, rings of black liquid seeping over the side. "It must look really nice."

May nodded slowly. She was unable to grasp her cup, unable to speak. She closed her eyes, then, feeling with her fingers through her hair, she unpinned one bobby pin, then another, then another. It was as if her whole body was being unleashed as the pressure of each pin disappeared. Strands of hair fell against her face. She released a large pin at the center, and the mass of her hair fell to her shoulders, down her back, over her arms. Clutching her bobby pins in her fingers, she felt Mark's hand grasp hers.

* * *

As the August night cooled and the party dwindled to seven, the guests moved inside, to the den, around a cold fireplace. The women shed their shoes and curled their bare feet under their thighs or inside their sundresses; the men stretched their legs far out in front of them, as if they had been cramped before with too little space. The party lapsed into a peaceful, if somewhat tired, silence as they listened to the chirp of crickets, first the males, asking, then the females, answering: a summer melody.

"Who knows a funny story?" Jean asked. "Let's hear a funny story."

"You're the comedian, Jean," Dave said.

"Oh, only ninth-graders laugh at my jokes. I know!" Jean reached toward May. "Tell us about your blind dates."

"Oh, a blind date! How fun!" Becky said.

May looked around, in the half-lit darkness, at the gleaming teeth and widened stares of her rapt audience. "I've sworn off them."

"May— c'mon," Jean said. "Tell us about the lawyer. It's hysterical."

May waited to see if Mark would intervene, but he stared vaguely in her direction, his faint, expectant smile mimicking his guests'.

"Really, there's not much to it," May said. She slid her hand through her hair, then flicked it over her shoulder. "I had a lunch date set up with a lawyer that a friend knew."

"Tell them why it was lunch," Jean said.

When May had told this story to Jean, May had embellished the rudeness, had pointed out ironies with an easy self-deprecating humor. She didn't think she could do it tonight. "My vast experience in this area," May said, "has taught me to make these test-runs as short as possible."

"That way she doesn't get stuck with the nerd for a whole evening," Jean said.

"So I arrive at the restaurant five minutes late – not even – and he's already ordered."

"No!" Becky said, and even the husbands chuckled, relieved they wouldn't have to defend mankind. The lawyer was obviously a clod.

"May was nice enough to stay for lunch. I would've left. So keep going," Jean said.

"To make conversation, I tell him about the minor accident I was in the week before. Only to find out he's an accident attorney. We spend our entire time talking about tort law—"

"A fascinating lunch topic," Jean said, inserting the comments May had included when she had told Jean the story.

"—and why I should sue, and why I should hire him to do it. He gives me his card, and calls me five times in four days, to see if he can represent me."

Jean's laughter burst out, taking on its hysterical note, and everyone began laughing, as much at Jean as at May's story, except for May and Mark, who smiled politely. Jean gasped for air. "The most phone calls May had gotten after a blind date," she squealed, then continued laughing again, pealing up the scale, as extreme, as inappropriate, as always. Breathless, she squeaked out, "Tell them about the Indian."

"An American Indian?" Becky asked.

"No," Jean said, "he was from—"

"Jean." Mark's level voice silenced her. He picked up an empty bottle of Rioja. "More wine?"

Dave changed the subject to baseball as Mark left to find another bottle. After a moment, May ignored her instinct and offered to help. She took orders for soda and walked through the dark dining room and into the kitchen. She found Mark standing in front of the sink, leaning on his arms.

He turned when he heard her. She saw his rugged face weighed down, cheeks sloping, eyelids puffed and heavy, and then, again, she saw Mark. "May." He smiled crookedly; his blue eyes cleared. May retrieved three glasses from the cabinet and a bucket of ice from the freezer as Mark, beside her, began uncorking the wine.

"She knows—" May said, her voice faint, her words trailing off. "Doesn't she?"

Mark spoke slowly, the rhythm of his voice matching the turn of his hand. "I don't think so."

"Then what was that?"

"Subconscious. A coincidence, perhaps."

"She's going to figure it out."

"No." Mark wrapped a kitchen towel around the bottle.

May threw ice cubes in the last glass. "How can you say that?"

"She'll figure me out. She already suspects. I may have to tell her— not who, but what." Mark grabbed her hands suddenly. "I'm sorry," he said. May slipped her fingers from his palms. "Your hands are freezing."

"It's the ice," May said. He waited silently while she filled two glasses with Coke and a third with water, then he took the water glass, which was hers.

"Women expect it of men," Mark said as they walked back to the den. "They don't expect it of other women."

May sat through the next half-hour only so she wouldn't cause a scene by leaving right away. She glanced occasionally at Mark; the worn-down husband, the overburdened lover, the heavy-lidded stranger did not reappear, yet it was those men who remained with her. During their six months together, Mark's calm confidence had convinced May that their deception, stripped of its surroundings, held beauty, purity, even innocence. At the heart of their flawed romance was something solid – a clear crystal, like a diamond – that May held onto for strength, for endurance, when she was alone. She grasped for it now and found nothing. There was Mark, talking, smiling, inches away from her, yet she grasped at nothing.

The party broke up, everyone standing to leave almost at once. May rose with the other guests, but Jean stopped her. "May's going to stay a little longer, Sweetie, won't you?" She grabbed May's arm, squeezing it tightly, almost hurting her. May couldn't resist Jean; she nodded her head. Jean hugged and kissed the other guests good night, and nudged Mark to walk them to their cars. She leaned out the screened door, waving. When she came back inside, Jean's smile faded one forced piece at a time. She grabbed May's arm again, but this time as if she needed the support to walk. "Sit with me a bit, in the screened porch," Jean said, leading May even as she leaned on her. "I hate the emptiness after a party. It makes me feel— bereft."

They sat in the dark, in separate chaises longues, listening to the crunching of stones as the guests ambled to their cars. May could hear the even keel of Mark's voice over the others, its rhythm warm and steady. If May closed her eyes she could feel his words caressing her skin.

"I never understood why you didn't marry Tim," Jean said.

May sensed the rest of Jean's question: Why she hadn't avoided the blind dates, the unasked questions, the faulty assumptions.

May gave her a pat answer. "I wasn't ready."

"Do you regret it?" May began to bristle until she realized there was no malice in Jean's voice. Curiosity, even fear, but no malice. May counted the things she would have escaped by marrying Tim. A near-rape by a man she met at a party. Christmas Eve the year after Tim left. Mark's voice. Mark's rough-smooth hands. Mark's breath on her neck as he slept, not often enough, beside her.

"No," May said. "I don't."

They listened to the slam of car doors and the rush of motors indicating the guests were departing in earnest. "I wasn't ready either," Jean said.

"You?"

"Me. Little Jeannie the school teacher. Can't you see me on an archeological dig? Discovering new fauna in the rain forest?"

It wasn't the Jean she had known all her life, and May tried to picture this other Jean – face thick with tan, hair cut bluntly, for who had time for things such as style? A Jean pushed to the edge of life. May couldn't envision her.

The night was silent again, as silent as a country night can be, with an underbrush of owls and raccoons and deer always threatening to burst forth but seldom doing so.

"Do you?" May asked. "Regret it?"

Jean laughed, but it wasn't her contagious, hysterical laugh. It was cut short, swallowed, like a pill. "Of course not," she said.

They heard the screen door slam, then Mark's heavy footsteps in the kitchen. Glasses clinked as they were rinsed and placed in the dishwasher. "Oh, May," Jean said. May was sure it was the confession she had been trying, desperately, to avoid: Mark is so distant now, she doesn't know what's wrong, she can't cajole him out of it, he's only normal around other people, around May. Or perhaps Jean was waiting patiently for her to confess, or hoping, breathless, that May would keep silent. They sat together in the dark room. One of them sighed. "Nothing is perfect," Jean said. "Is it?"

She tried to make out Jean in the shadows and could see only the spike of her hair. She wondered if Jean would trade with her: May's career, May's freedom, for Mark. Would she? Yet even then May would be missing the same things she missed now with Mark: the crunch of stones on a driveway being her stones, the slam of a door being her door, the hum of her own house, her own husband, her own life. She didn't want Jean's life. She never had. Now, she wondered it Jean would give it up as well.

Mark's shadow appeared in the doorway. "Dark enough in here?" he asked.

"Don't turn on the light," Jean said evenly. "Sweetie."

Mark adopted a hick accent. "How'm I supposed to know which woman's mine?" He grinned stupidly in the dark.

"Over there," May said, waving her arm in Jean's direction. "Jean's over there."

The One I Will

When I meet him, I look like my plain self – wearing loose jeans and a t-shirt, hair bunched in a ponytail, not a smudge of make-up. I am in line to renew my license, have been told to sit in the waiting area for my turn. He, I overhear as I read the magazine I had the foresight to bring, is ordering a passport photo, standing against a white wall in front of a camera. He smiles for his picture, waits for the SNAP! of the flash. And as his face lights up, his smile hooking as he begins to feel foolish grinning, grinning, grinning for the camera, I see he'd be the perfect victim.

I nod when he sits a few seats away from me but continue to read my *Time*. He will not notice me the way I look today. Today, I am the type of girl he might chat with a while, see as sweet and intelligent, and leave behind with hardly a thought. I am the type they say they want to marry and of course don't, because they don't marry the marriage type, or don't marry at all. I am used to this and no longer care. I get my due.

He's looking around for something to read. The pickings are slim but he's restless. He must occupy his mind with whatever's nearby. He settles on, of all things, *Seventeen*. He leans forward, both elbows on his knees in a sitting version of the "ready" stance in baseball. What will he read? "Seven

Exercises to Tone Your Tummy?" "How to Tell Your Boyfriend You're Ready?" He leafs through it then quickly puts it on the table, pats it as if he needs to be sure it will stay there. He looks around to see if anyone noticed and catches me watching.

"A subscriber?" I ask.

He blushes so his face is lit from beneath in a pink glow that makes his skin look so warm I want to touch it. His smile hooks again. "Think I read that one already."

It's his chin that gets me. It's a square tough-guy chin that juts out when he walks to the counter to choose his photo, when he readjusts his body in his seat. His chin is not, at four o'clock, completely clean shaven. Blond whiskers are asserting themselves through his tan, which isn't a tan so much as the golden hue of his skin. It matches the amber of his eyes, the gold of his hair. Yet he is no Apollo. He's short, a little stocky. His smile is not braces-perfect, his two eye-teeth higher than the others. His top lip peaks in the middle, like he's thinking of a question.

Then it's my turn to be photographed. I hand him my *Time* ("Hey, thanks!") then go to stand against the white wall as if for a "most wanted" photo, wishing I could bring some color to my winter-pale face. I look over and he's already engrossed in my magazine, not thinking of the invisible girl who lent it to him. If I had bright red lips, he'd see me. If I were wearing a tight shirt, black and silky, jeans so snug he could make out my crotch— then he'd look. They all look. I know.

This is some consolation as I sit again and he doesn't glance up right away, until he remembers he has borrowed my *Time*. I introduce myself as he hands it back. He introduces himself. I tell him he has a nice name and he blushes as if I'd said, "You know, you've got a cute ass."

He does. Shapely underneath his loose-fitting suit pants, it compares favorably with the others I have coaxed home the last few months, using my newly discovered tools of trade. I used to be ashamed of my body – my too-thick calves, the hidden roll of my stomach, my small, beaky nose, watchful, smart. I used to compress my breasts into too-tight bras to make them look smaller, to make me look thinner. Then I realized that flesh is best, beauty is breast. It's all I needed. Now I show off my body. In winter I am the sweater girl – cashmere makes my breasts soft and inviting. In summer I am so sheer they can just see the pink rounds of my nipples. I no longer worry about a tad extra flesh on my arms, my thighs – if it is bare, that's all that matters.

My license, his passport, are ready at the same time, and we walk up to the counter together to pay our bills. He makes pleasant chit-chat with the blond behind the counter, practically a teenager, twice as appealing. We walk out at the same time, and I ask him, as a girl in the overlarge t-shirt he'll never remember, as the curious woman with the fading face:

"Where are you going?"

I mean, Where is he traveling, what exotic locale does he need a passport for? Is it a honeymoon in Mallorca, a business trip to Munich, a hike in Nepal? Where are you going? But his eyes darken for a minute, he steps away from me, and then I see it. He thinks I mean, Where are you going right now? His eyes clear as he catches his mistake. He laughs at his misunderstanding. "Oh!" he says. "Nowhere yet. I mean, I have a new job, I may need a passport— "

"No," I say. "I mean, where are you going right now?"

He's new in town, so we go for a drink at a bar I choose because it's easy to find. I feel weaponless in this chain restaurant with the clever menu, unarmed with the artillery I use to capture men. I don't even have Chapstick with me; I'm wearing my faded cotton bra so stretched it sags. But this seems like the right place to take him, the kind of place to go for a drink. The noise of the bar covers up our silences. We can concentrate on flagging down a bartender, figuring out what to order. He confides in me.

"This is where I ate last night," he says.

"Oh, I'm sorry." And I am. The food isn't very good for one night, let alone two. "There's tons of places—"

"It's fine. I just had nachos."

"A bachelor's dinner," I say, not meaning to be nosy. There's no wedding ring, not that I usually care.

"Well, I can try something more substantial tonight."

"Dangerous," I say. I let the word hang a bit before I explain. "Nachos are the high point. It goes downhill from there."

It's truer than I meant it. I think of my evenings with men, men cocky and a little drunk, men pushy with their hands on my arms and legs, men gentle with mock-tender gazes. Oh yes, downhill after the nachos. It's truer than I meant it.

So you ask: why do I bother? Why go along with the post-nachos, post-dinner, post-date disappointments? Well, I don't deal, anymore, in disappointment. I am just a tease. I have not slept with a single one.

Oh, yes, I visit their bedrooms. I have drinks on their couch, I grope in the car, on the beach, on the rug, on the desk in the office – and then I stop. Oh no, I say. Not that. I say I'm sick, I'm hungry, I'm menstruating, my baby-sitter needs to get home, I'm not doing anything without a condom – oops. Sorry.

Besides, as my grandmother used to say: they won't buy the cow if the milk is free.

I can't push all of them that far. Some wouldn't hear my female protests; some wouldn't care. That kind I duck out on early. I say after drinks that I have an appointment, after dinner that I'm meeting a friend, after dessert that I have to pick up my boyfriend at the airport. Sometimes I just say, Well, gotta run. But usually it's safe to go home with them if I want to. Often I want to. Often I tease myself – will I, won't I? Will I, won't I? – into their beds. But— I won't.

This is my revenge. For the times I was left waiting, left wondering, left empty-hearted. Trace it back to sixth-grade, when I blamed my shoes, to junior high, blame my hair, to high school, blame the weight, to college, blame their youth, to work, singles groups, Club Meds, blame me, blame me, blame me.

Finally I blamed them.

* * *

He begins to talk about his new job. Men's jobs, men's lives, always make good talking points. And he seems nice enough. He even gives me a little flutter in my stomach, if I let him. He asks about what movies I've loved, what my favorite food is, if I have a favorite food scene in a movie. Will I, won't I, will I, won't I? I long for the costume that makes me look like someone else, for the costume that allows me to decide.

My guess is he isn't abandoning any girlfriend at home by moving here. He's exploding with information, with stuff to share. He's been hired by a local power company to research solar alternatives. It's part of a deal with a regulatory agency unhappy about safety violations at a nuclear plant, but he's as excited as a boy at his first day of Little League. He's convinced that when nuclear power companies start to look to solar energy, it's the dawning of a new world.

"But aren't you sort of working for the enemy?" I ask. "Do they even want you to succeed?"

He gets serious all of a sudden. "I've thought a lot about that. Am I just a token gesture? But I think they want to make it work. That's what's wonderful about solar energy – it's cheaper for them too. No costly clean-up. No bricks of nuclear waste to hide in a desert somewhere."

"They could indoctrinate you."

He smiles. "I'll indoctrinate them."

I might believe it. He's leaning closer to me now, his butt just hanging onto the bar stool as it tips toward me. And even though I'm not in black, even though I look like just another nice girl, I let my legs dangle near his, my knee not quite touching his thigh.

Was this all I needed? A little forwardness to complement my personality, my brains? Maybe I didn't need the red lipstick and tight skirt. Maybe I just never knew, before, how to flirt. I was too nice, too sincere. I didn't send the right signals – didn't know to send signals at all. Tonight, it all comes easily – the intimate lean forward, the staring into eyes, the touch on an elbow or knee. It all seems so natural.

"So the passport means you can look into solar energy in Paris?" I ask. "Do some research in the Bahamas?"

"Naaa," he says, the stool tipping precariously on two legs. "I mean, I might need it for work, but I want to travel some."

I am pleased with this. It was disappointing to think he was getting a passport because he was told to. I ask him where he wants to travel and he lists a zillion places – was there anywhere he didn't want to go? – then mentions Jerusalem.

"It seems like such a— vortex," he says. "So many cultures. It's just— such a piece of history. How about you?"

"Egypt," I say, then I'm embarrassed when I realize how close it is to Jerusalem.

He grins. "Same neighborhood. Why?"

"Pyramids."

He nods, as if I'd said something profound, something worth puzzling over. "Maybe," he says, eyeing me tentatively, shy all of a sudden in this low-key singles bar, "we're hoping to find some sort of wisdom there."

I mimic his nod, wanting him to know I'm taking him seriously, but I'm too struck with him, too conscious of his intent gaze, to come up with a thoughtful response. "Maybe," I say.

It's enough. He smiles quick, leans way forward, drums his fingers on my knee – lightly, barely touching, his almost-touch sending a shiver up my spine – then sits back. "I'll meet you there."

The check arrives and he picks it up, doesn't allow me to protest. "Expense," he says, and we sit a little awkward as we both realize that wasn't the suavest thing for him to say. He catches me trying not to smile. "You know," he says, blushing under that left hook of a grin, "I'd like to invite you over but— I'm still staying at a hotel and—"

And that would be tacky. I am touched by his consideration. He thinks I'm a nice girl. Nice girls don't do hotel rooms.

"We could have a drink in the lobby," he says.

Oh— For the first time, I think: I have him.

"Your living room?" I ask.

"My gracious, immense living room. I live quietly there, just me and my butlers. A few friends— I mean, guests—"

He loses his concentration, his gaze darting away when I catch him staring at my face. And though I've never invited the others to my apartment, not daring to, not wanting to, not trusting anyone, I hear myself ask:

"How about my living room?"

* * *

He follows me in his car to my apartment. I don't give him directions; he is reliant on me. For a moment I am tempted to lose him – old habits, old fears. I speed a little to see if he'll catch up, to test how much he wants me. I turn without signaling. He keeps pace. The headlights of his rental stay close; he shoots his highs once to be friendly. Yes, I have him, yet I wonder, wonder, wonder if this one will be different.

Because I want this one to be different. I've wanted them all – almost – to be different. I didn't start out seeking revenge. I began by chance. There was no reason for my sudden transformation. A blind date I'd had the night before a black leather mini caught my eye on my way to a dressing room, a practical navy dress in hand, had held possibility. I didn't know yet, when I asked the saleslady if I could wear the skirt home, liking the way its belled shape hugged my body, that he would be another prospect that never called a second time. I thought the looks from men that evening, as I waited for a girlfriend in a bar, were my imagination, that the man who approached me before she arrived was a fluke. Until I ran a non-scientific experiment and it happened again. And again.

I didn't get any invitations home – not at first. I didn't know yet how to act – didn't know that body language had to accompany bodywear. And then I bewitched one. He was tall and a little overweight. He had a big red drinking face, though he didn't drink much that night, and a loud laugh. He thought he was funny. He was. But on my way to the Ladies Room I found myself sneaking outside instead. I went home by myself, slept by myself. I kept waking up to see the leather mini hanging on the closet door, a ghostly half-body, my lure and shield. I kept smelling the smoky bar on my hair, kept imagining the scent that the smoke covered up – the scent of sweaty bodies, male bodies – desire pulling me to them, repulsion pushing me away.

"Hey speedster," he says when we reach my place.

"Was I driving too fast?" I ask. I try to sound like this is how I drive, this is how I live, this is me.

Upstairs, I offer him a drink but he opts for water. I serve it in a scotch glass, sit beside him on the couch with a Perrier, closer to him than I might have sat a year ago, farther than I might have last night.

"Have you gone apartment hunting yet?"

"Not yet," he says.

We are out of small talk and have something else on our minds. I sit sideways, facing him, one leg bent on the couch. He meets my gaze, looks away, meets my gaze, looks away.

I stand up. This maybe yes, maybe no hesitation doesn't happen to me anymore. I look at the CDs piled on my stereo for something to play— something to do. I don't know what mood to set. I don't know how to follow through. It would be so easy to yawn hugely, to look at him with sleepy eyes and say, Oh, I have a—

Then he yawns, mouth wide, wide open so I spot a few fillings inside my non-Apollo. He makes a little yelping yawn noise then shakes his head. "Long day," he says, and I think, No, no, no, don't leave me, no.

He stands next to me to look at the music and I let him choose, let him set the mood. Stan Getz. Perhaps not all is lost and we sit down again on the couch. I stare at him next to me and this time he doesn't look away. When he closes his eyes I know he's going to kiss me.

I wish I could say it was sweet from the start, but at first all I taste is beer and onion. It is never pleasant to kiss somebody for the first time. It's a little like landing in a foreign country. The air smells fishy. The chicken tastes salty. You can't read the menu. Then he loosens my ponytail as if he'd been wanting to do that all night, splays his fingers through my hair. His tongue darts into my mouth once, startling me, twice, getting used to it, retreats. I wait for it to return, search for it with my own tongue. He is beginning to taste like a person. I can feel the thickness of his lips. His tongue darts once, startling me, twice, used to it, retreats.

I think he's been practicing.

And so have I. I feel so ready for him, as if all the men I've met, all the men I've flirted with, all the men I've kissed, all the men I've almost slept with, were one long continuing string of foreplay, preparing me for this man, preparing me for him. All the dinners I've eaten, all the glasses of wine, all the after-dinner drinks in outdoor bars and hotel lobbies and strangers' bedrooms were a woman's way of getting used to things. All the walks along the—

But you want me to come to my point, don't you? To the culmination of my story. You want to know if, this time... Are you too shy to ask now? I'll say it for you: You want to know if we had sex. You want to know if the way he lost his train of thought when he caught my eye touched me in a way that nudging hands and intruding lips had not.

What if I told you we fell in love and lived merrily ever after? Can you picture me in white silk, white roses held in my arm like a child, a lace blusher softening the light until my face shimmers as I walk up the aisle, a virgin angel?

But would this man fall to such a mundane fate? A man who ordered a passport without knowing exactly where he wanted to go? Wasn't he ready for adventure, excitement? Maybe I gave him one night of excitement. Yes, more than I gave my other gentleman. So the man with the passport came over, had his book stamped with my name or face or whatever detail of me memory will not allow him to forget, and left – never called, never wrote. Is that how it went?

Oh, it was far worse than that.

We did not sleep together that night. His yawns overcame him, he kissed me again, politely, and left. But he phoned when he got settled in town, not knowing anyone else, I suppose, not knowing what else to do, and we had sex then, and then again, and then again, for two years, until we saw each other every day. We had lunches and dinners around our sex, had weekends and vacations and yes a trip to the Middle East around our sex, had shopping trips and movies and tennis and parental visits and cooking and— All this we worked around our sex. Of course we slept together. He left strands of hair on my pillow, kicked my sheets onto the floor. I drooled on his chest, on the t-shirt he wore to bed, tucked neatly into his underpants. Sometimes at night, to sleep better, we would unconsciously roll away from each other, but in the morning, before he was fully awake, still flushed and dazed like a child, his thick arm pulled me close again, as if he thought he'd lost me in the night.

Yes, we had a— relationship— and after all that, after two years, a month and eleven days, he said—

He had come to pick me up for dinner, and I kissed him at the door and hugged him and chattered about my lunch with Julia and showed him the earrings I bought my mother that day and dangled the ones I had bought for myself. I told him how I'd finally made it to the camera shop to print a few photos from our last trip as he sat down and accepted a scotch. He sipped and humphed and held my hand but then took his away and wouldn't look at me and said—

Well, you all know what he said. It's an old story by now. The modern man who isn't ready, who says it isn't you, who hasn't seen enough of— I don't need to tell you, do I? It's way too familiar to repeat. Let's just say his passport didn't sport enough stamps.

And so I have returned to the coffee shops and museums, book stores and art galleries, parks and street festivals. I ensnare them as they flip through CDs at Tower Records; as they watch their daughter on the swing, I set my trap for revenge. Because the man who I thought would prove me wrong has proved me right. And I was so right. What I learned works better than ever. My lips are redder, my cheeks pinker, sometimes I streak my hair auburn or blond. Of course, I have to choose my victims more carefully now, because while I have dieted, gone veggie, exercised and begun a regimen of Retin-A, I am a little older now, and that can make a difference. Some younger ones are turned on by an older woman but others will give me a stare – amused, sarcastic, or just blank – that my red nails and black chamois do not always protect me against.

But don't worry. My three-pronged lure of sex, sex and sex still attracts. I let my body flutter in their sight. I am not real, but metal and plastic, make-up and feathers, a mirage that brings them out, brings them closer, brings them almost— then disappears. Oh, no. Not that. Except— one night, I spot a blond with a crooked smile who's too shy at first to meet my gaze. Maybe he asks me a few questions; maybe he answers a few of mine. When we leave the bar for the thick summer air, he walks me to my car and kisses me good night. I feel his hand rest, gentle, curious, on my back. His thumb explores the concave of my spine. Then he says good night, holds up the number he's written on a scrap of paper, hot and wrinkled in his hand. Him, I let go.

The City of Brotherly Something

At the rehearsal for her father's wedding, Tree stood alone in the front pew wondering what exactly was being rehearsed. The minister spoke lightly, almost comically, the familiar phrases tossed about the spare Congregational church like softballs in a backyard game of catch. Did the meaning behind the words, at this late hour, need practice? Tree missed the somber tone of the parish priest whom her family had grown up complaining about— wished her father hadn't agreed so easily to a Protestant ceremony, though she hadn't given it a thought until just then.

"And do you, Vincent..." the minister sing-songed.

"I *will*," her father answered, never one to miss a pass.

Their sparse crowd laughed, all except Tree. How quickly it would become, I do. It was she who needed the rehearsing – practice smiling, practice looking celebratory, practice giving her father a kiss without holding back. Tears could be misconstrued, but not coldness. It wasn't loyalty to her mother, not entirely – her mother had died years ago. She just never thought her father would *marry* Martha, who seemed like merely the perfect date. She tried not to think of David, how his quick hijack of a laugh might fill any void her silence might create. How much easier this would have been with him.

The groom turned to kiss the bride. He was too formally dressed as usual. Even Martha was wearing something cool enough the take Philadelphia's summer swelter. But no, her father had to keep up appearances and wear long sleeves, a tie and a dark jacket. He did look handsome, even at sixty-three. Her mother had always pooh-poohed her husband's looks, called him Prince Charming in a way that deprecated his charms. Yet she admitted, one time after she became ill, talking and talking as if the teenaged Teresa were the one who needed soothing, that seeing him could make her legs tremble if he caught her unawares – if he surprised her in the garden, if she ran into him, as she sometimes had, covering a press conference downtown. She'd said it like a confession – worried, after all those years, that she had fallen in love with just a pretty face.

The pretend vows, the pretend wedding over, the couple turned and walked down the aisle. Martha – blonde, Main Line Martha – might be the spouse to cause delightful shivers now. Teresa suspected that good looks were a prerequisite for any man Martha might date, a fact duly noted then forgotten. *Handsome? Well, of course.* She carried her father on her arm as casually as she wore that delicate pearl choker around her neck.

"Honey!" Her father hugged her and held her to him a minute. He whispered in her ear. "How's my Tree?"

"You looked pretty comfortable up there."

"Oh, I put on a good act!"

All this was what she and David had wanted to avoid a year ago – at least, that was the reason he had used. Now, she saw the purpose of it all – the rehearsal, the rehearsal dinner, the choosing of flowers and hymns. Who would go through with it if they weren't sure? It winnowed out the tame of heart, or maybe forced them to be brave.

* * *

David and Tree were planning to elope the morning he never showed up. She sat atop the high, gracious steps that led to her brownstone apartment, wearing the white sleeveless dress that he had always liked so much, carrying a sheer, white sweater she had to buy specially for the occasion because you never knew when the weather would turn in San Francisco. She waited for him in that dress that was and wasn't a wedding dress and never got impatient, enjoying the moment before the moment he would arrive and they'd be off to City Hall. It hit her all at once that he wouldn't show. For more than an hour she sat on the wide cement landing that she would always remember as an altar, a small tree on either side of her like kneeling altar boys, Tree left sitting polished and gleaming on the doorstep like a chalice, the gifts untouched inside her.

Three months and three thousand miles later, the electric sign atop the Philadelphia Electric Co. building glared into her new apartment like a harmless peeping Tom. PENN HOMECOMING – WELCOME ALUMS, the yellow letters as tall and wide as the windows in her factory-converted studio. She'd come home without him— to Philadelphia, to a job at the website for the newspaper she'd grown up wanting to write for, sister to the paper where her mother had worked. Yet it didn't feel like home. The apartment was dark and empty, all her belongings on a truck somewhere between San

Francisco and Philadelphia. As night fell she realized she didn't even have a lamp. The only light was the overhead in the bathroom, in the back of the loft that was her bedroom. She sat on the toilet for a while, the lid down, reading a newspaper, too tired to venture out alone into the city.

When she wandered downstairs to retrieve her sleeping bag she saw the Peco sign again. PECO ENERGY. IS HERE. TO STAY. She'd looked at the apartment during the daytime only, not thinking about the nighttime Peco sign. She stood holding her rolled-up sleeping bag, waiting for the letters to wrap around so she could read the punch line. NO DOUBT. She waited again. Was that it? Just as she was about to give up, the sign added – ABOUT IT – as if it knew she'd been waiting. It felt like company, a slow-talking guest who'd hang around a little longer than Tree wanted.

When the phone rang with the same ring it'd had in California, Tree expected it to be her father. Instead, it was David.

"Hey, Tree, how's it going?" he said as if he still called every day. After weeks of arguments and tears and long explanations that explained nothing, sex that ended in more arguments and more tears, they'd stopped trying. Stopped speaking. She remembered beating down on his bony shoulders one night before they broke it off, wishing she could pound what had happened out of him and out of her. She'd never even called to say she was moving, figured he'd learn about it somehow. "It's David," he added quickly.

She was too shocked to do anything but act normal. "Hi," she said. "I'm in Philly." She tried to breathe in, breathe out, as she told him about her new job, the apartment, her sister Holly's new role in an off-Broadway play. "I've got a view of the Peco sign," she said.

"That's nice."

"No, I mean my view *is* the Peco sign." David had grown up in Philly too – had gone to the boys' school in Haverford where her father was headmaster – so when she said 23rd and Walnut, he could picture it exactly. None of their California friends could.

The sign flashed at her. "10.22p.m," she said. "46 degrees."

She told him about her father's engagement, announced the weekend before. David sounded more stunned than Tree had. She realized she was pleased. Though it wasn't much to throw in an ex-boyfriend's face, news about your father getting married.

"What, to Martha?"

"Mm-hmmm."

"Huh." He laughed a quick, guttural laugh, like he was emitting something – hesitation, surprise, the new knowledge that he would no longer learn such things first-hand. "She's pretty good-looking, you know, for fifty-whatever. Vince is doing okay."

"Great," Tree said. "I'm glad they're getting married then. I'm just thrilled."

"Oh, Tree. C'mon. You're not upset about it, are you?" David was silent then, the way he was when he realized he should have known something. "They've been seeing each other for years."

After they hung up, she wandered around her apartment in the dark, from the empty living room to the partially separate and empty dining room to the kitchen to the living room, up the stairs to her empty loft bedroom and back down the stairs to the living room until finally she grabbed her jacket and walked outside, air cool but moist, 46 degrees. She headed south toward Old City until she was running, panting, until some sense that it was midnight and raining and maybe dangerous to be rambling around by herself sent her home.

* * *

It was the things she had hated about David that she missed the most. Petty things that had driven her nuts – she knew they were petty even then. The way her covers would become a jumble from David's tossing and turning and pulling – and now, she walked out of the bathroom each morning to the sight of her neat bed, unmade but barely ruffled. In a fit of anger, she had thrown out the pillow that had been his. Her comforter hung limply off her one pillow like a sleeve over a missing limb.

He began calling every other night. She thought of eighteen reasons why, none of them convincing. He was apologizing, assuaging his guilt, making sure she was okay. Who knew? Probably not David. It occurred to her he could just be trying to be nice, trying to be a friend. But what kind of friend calls the woman he stood up at the altar? A friend might just fade away.

There were rules. He always called at night. He never called on Saturday (was he not in? Did he not want to admit it if he were?). If he wouldn't be home, he'd call that afternoon and leave a message.

She never phoned him. She realized the skipped nights might be an opening for her to call. Was that his design? Would her calling him be a signal that things between them were even again – that he had paid his fine? She didn't think she would ever call him, not even in an emergency. She didn't want to need him – his phone calls, their talks, any remnants of their love, or whatever it had been. She didn't like calling it "love" anymore. But what was it, if not love? Well, she supposed it was something.

* * *

Her father and Martha settled on a six-month engagement. It was silly, really, for two people their age to go through this waiting period, but Martha wanted to choose a restaurant, order flowers, and maintain a sense of propriety. Tree was grateful for every minute of it. She spent more time with her father than a single 31-year-old woman should. Fridays became their night. She'd go to the house she'd grown up in to have dinner. At first, Martha joined them, playing the role of hostess in a home none of them thought of as hers. Then she began making other plans. Tree didn't know if she was giving them father-daughter time, or feeling put out.

She felt her mother's absence at these dinners more than she had in years. It was just Tree and her father again, the way it had been after her mother had died and Holly had gone off to college. Her mother could dominate a conversation even in listening mode, and so Tree heard herself talk about things her mother, more than her father, would find interesting – gossip from the paper, controversies over stories, a new play in town. Her father was interested, too, but it was her mother she was telling and he was responding to.

One night in June, Martha stayed for dinner. Both her father and Martha could chit-chat well, so the evening was effortless. It was their most shared trait.

"A bridal shower!" her father said gleefully, chuckling. "They threw me a bridal shower, my boys."

Her father was the only man she knew who was given

showers. It was her mother's word for them. When Holly and Tree were born, the boys at the school on their own initiative held parties to celebrate the girls' arrival. She had heard so many stories about the pink ribbons and the party favors wrapped in pink netting and the pink tissue paper they'd hung on the walls of his headmaster's office like they were re-papering the place, Tree almost felt she could remember it – her first memory a blur of pink.

"It was very sweet of them," Martha said. "To hold a—" she hesitated "—party for us. Don't you think?"

"Sure," Tree said,

"They threw me a bridal shower." Her father was still grinning at the thought of it, at the merriment of the boys. "Of course, you can guess who was behind it. I mean, who else—"

"Vin," Martha said firmly to Tree's father. "Vin, dear, can you pass me the butter?"

Her father cleared his throat. Martha buttered a slice of sourdough, using a ceramic-handled butter knife, ivory and green, that Tree had never seen before.

"David set it up?" she said. "Dad?"

"Vin," Martha said again. Vince, Tree thought. His name is Vince.

"Martha, it wasn't – it shouldn't be a secret. He's mentoring one of the boys in eighth grade – Tree, you know how alums do that, visit when in town, e-mail. So David mentored him on throwing me a shower." Her father chuckled as if David were still thirteen.

"And he went through with it," Tree said. "No cold feet. It's rather amazing."

No one laughed. She realized it wasn't funny. Tree missed her mother right then more than she had in years. Her mother would have laughed. She would have made a better joke so Tree could laugh.

Martha left to meet a friend for drinks, a plan she hadn't mentioned until after dinner. Tree thought about leaving, too, abandoning her father to summer dusk and the stillness of the air. Somehow she couldn't. She helped him clean up. Her father walked quietly from the dining room table to the kitchen, table to kitchen, scraping off dishes and handing them to her, emptied but still runny with dinner. They fell into a rhythm of his giving, her taking, rinsing, clinking into the dishwasher just as he was back to hand her another dish. "My turn," he said when it was time to do the pots. He took over at the sink as she brushed up crumbs with her hand, wiped table and counter, put on water for tea. It was soothing, their old routine. How strange it must have been, after she went off to college, for him to do it alone.

They settled into the screened-in porch with mugs of tea and cookies, her father's weakness. The cat, relegated to the porch because of Martha's allergies, made herself comfortable on Tree's lap. She petted the top of her striped gray head, between the ears, where she knew the cat liked being pet.

"I'm sorry, Tree. I'd gotten wind of it, I admit that. But I didn't know how to say, Don't throw me a shower. It seemed so— innocent."

She didn't answer him. She shut her eyes for a moment to the world she'd grown up in, but the image of the white wicker loveseat, the green floral cushions, the old radio with the little orange "on" button, remained.

"He's a little like a son, you know. They all are."

The cat kneaded her stomach, the pushy pads of her feet burrowing into her, her claws not quite snagging on her shirt.

"Do you not understand what he did to me?"

"I don't think he understood, Tree."

"Oh, c'mon." She shook her head, waved her hand.

"Do you miss him?" her father asked. "Do you miss David still."

"What do you think?"

"Would you give him another chance?"

In the distance she heard the dull roar of I-95. It was worse at night, when the clouds were low. She wondered if David had apologized to her father. He hadn't to her.

"Did he ask you for one?" she asked.

He laughed softly. "I'm not his agent, you know. I don't negotiate for him."

"Then what?"

"I just think he might have made a stupid mistake, and not known how to correct it. A kid mistake. A *boy's* mistake."

Dad and his boys. He could forgive them anything, she thought.

Tree nibbled on her cookie – shortbread – and realized it was homemade. Martha and her secret gifts. Her mother had made horrible cookies. She never left them in long enough. Holly as a kid began putting them back in the oven, then she'd forget and let them burn. It was a family trait, not being able to make cookies.

Her father pressed on. "Maybe he needed to wait."

She thought of her wait on the steps – the taunting blue sky, her girlish dress. Two construction workers carrying hard hats had walked by, tan faces creased and stubbled, and smirked at her. She had sat on the landing, hands tucked under her thighs, her feet slowly tap-tapping on the step below. The silver high heels with the Cinderella look that she hadn't been able to resist made a teasing sound like dancing. Tap. Tap. Did she really think she'd tramp around San

Francisco in these? The silly dress— why had she worn white? At some point, she went inside to change. She put on jeans and a t-shirt and her ugliest running shoes. Still she went out to wait for him, still she sat on the steps, unable to give up.

"You wouldn't have asked Mom to wait," she said. Growing up, she'd heard stories of their romance: their father sending chocolates, flowers, a blueberry pie from her native New Hampshire. Once he showed up at a press conference she was covering. He'd known going up to her when she was working would be a fatal mistake, so he just stood where she could see him, a bushy handful of black-eyed Susans hiding his face.

"I waited for her."

The cat jumped down and switched to her father, as if it were following a schedule that gave each of them equal time. It stared back at Tree from her father's lap with an odd expression: a little stern, a little pleaful, a little apologetic.

"Why are you making me feel sorry for him?" she asked.

"That's not—" He re-crossed his legs. The cat rode the wave of her father shifting. "Honey, he was wrong. I know that. But has he asked you for another chance?"

She thought of David's phone calls, the consistent schedule, the reliable ring at ten o'clock every other night, his equanimous tone.

"I don't know," she said.

* * *

Her sister, Holly, skipping the rehearsal itself, arrived at the rehearsal dinner from New York with such a knockout date, even Martha must have noticed. He had a sculpted body and a sculpted face and hair blacker than his hip black glasses. Really, had she hired the guy? He was definitely hireable.

"Everything is just *perfect*," Holly gushed to Martha, giving her a hug and an Italian-style kiss – left cheek, right cheek – that left Martha smoothing her dress. To Tree, she said *sotto voce*, like the actress she was, "I can do this. I figure it's just twenty-two hours. Right? The best performance of my life." Then louder, "Sweet, sit between us." Then just soft enough so anyone could hear, "He's good enough to share, don't you think? He deserves two women on his arm."

The restaurant in downtown Philly was tasteful and reserved. The waiters seemed almost motionless as they slid from table to table with wine and water and, for Holly, a martini. Her mother had liked the Victor Café in South Philly for special occasions, a noisy, Italian place where the waiters occasionally put down their trays and broke into opera.

"How are my girls tonight? Hmmm?" Their father leaned over, kissed each of them on the cheek and left his arm, warm, on their shoulders. Once, "my girls" had included their mother.

"How are *you*?" Holly asked. Could her father hear her insinuation? Tree resisted the urge to tap her sister on the arm, reminder her to be good, to keep quiet. It would merely egg her on. "The man of the hour."

"Oh, I'm great. Isn't this fun? Amazing girls, amazing." He wandered off again, to the bar for a drink, nearly careening into his old friend Jack, in from Ohio. Tree wondered – how many drinks had he had? It wasn't like him.

"Is that like his fiftieth drink?" Holly asked. "Does he drink a lot now, Tree? You hadn't told me."

"Let it go, Holly," she said, as exasperated with herself as much as her sister. "He's getting married. He's fine."

A waiter – a woman, Tree noticed on second glance, thin with short hair so straight she looked like a boy – slipped salads in front of them as if she were giving them a secret file. "Who's the date?"

"My armor," Holly said. "My full-body armor. Isn't he beautiful?" They admired him for a moment as he swept up to the bar to get Tree a martini as well, Holly's idea. "He's in the play. Of course, I can't be sleeping with him. I've got to be fucking the fat middle-aged director."

Tree took this in, tried to remember what Holly had said about the director in the dozens of times, Tree now realized, she had dropped his name. Smart. Temperamental. Daughter— did he have a daughter who was an actress? Or was that a wife?

"No lectures, Tree. No point." Holly tilted her martini glass, nearly empty, and let the clear, glossy liquid brim, quivering, at the edge of the glass. "You'd like him, though. You would." She said it as if it were a warning. "He's brilliant. Mom would like him, too."

"She wouldn't want you to—"

"Well, duh," she said as if she were sixteen and they hadn't spent their high school years watching their mother return from doctors' offices paler and thinner and angrier – as if teenage sarcasm had been a luxury they could afford.

"You know," Holly said, "I always thought you stayed with David because Mom knew him."

"That's ridiculous. He was thirteen when she died."

As one of his father's favorites, David had been over the house a few times before their mother became ill. But he was two years younger than Tree. He wasn't even on the radar screen then as boy material.

The uber-date took his seat next to Holly, who put down her emptied glass and swigged from Tree's drink. "I'm stealing your martini," she said. "Sweet" she turned to him, "will you get us another one? We'll share this one."

She passed it to Tree, who took a sip, and passed it back.

"She knew him," Holly insisted. "They wouldn't have to be, you know, introduced."

As her sister dug a slender finger in for the olive, held it, glistening, before her mouth, then popped it in, Tree thought of the things their mother wouldn't know about them. Tree's job at the paper. Holly's blanking on her line on her first opening night. Tree's first news article. Or could her mother know more? Could she be watching from somewhere the way she'd told them their grandfather would be watching after he died? Maybe she would know things they wouldn't have told her – Holly's abortion. Tree's affair with a professor. Good things, too: the exact moment, watching him stand naked drinking a glass of water, that Tree knew she loved David. The water echoed in his throat, thumped his chest, rippled his stomach, twitched his penis; as he kept drinking she could almost see the water seep through him like a dye.

* * *

After dinner, as Holly circulated among relatives and family friends, Martha came to talk to Tree. "Teresa, you look marvelous tonight!" She took Holly's seat, so close their knees were almost touching. She placed her cup of tea on the table, fingered the lemon with her ringed hand.

"You're the one who looks marvelous." Tree found she meant it. Martha seemed relaxed. Her silken hair had curled a little wispy at her temples; her lipstick had worn off entirely. Perhaps her father would do Martha good.

"You're brave to show up by yourself." Martha spoke confidentially, girl-to-girl. "I did that for years."

"You've never been to a wedding alone!"

Martha tilted her head to the side and laughed. She tapped her mauve fingernail on her saucer then pointed it lightly at Tree. "It's true," she admitted. "But it doesn't help to bring someone you don't care about. It looks better but it doesn't help."

Tree watched Holly clutch the arm of her date, half flirtation, half need.

"But you know that already," Martha went on. "Your mother must have been very smart."

It was the first time Martha had ever mentioned Tree's mother so directly. It was oddly timed – something perhaps to get out of the way before the ceremony. Yet Tree found she was touched. Martha was trying. Music started up in the restaurant bar – a woman jazz singer. It sounded lazy and lovely and Tree wondered if her mother would like this place after all.

"Yes," she said. "She was."

"Is this hard for you, Tree?"

The song was a Billie Holiday, but the singer didn't try to sound like Billie. She let her full, rich tones deepen as the song slowed. Tree thought about what to say. She didn't, right then, want to lie. "My mother died a long time ago."

Martha nodded softly, brought her delicate hand up as if she might pat Tree's knee or cover her hand, then let it rest on the table. Her ring glittered in the light of the short candle. "I have to admit I was thinking of David."

"Oh." Tree found her wineglass and took a swallow. Across the room, she saw her father, in a circle of six people, slap the back of one of his friends. How much David would love this scene – the banter, the martinis, the silky dresses and ties, a crowd. Why in the world had she thought he'd want to elope?

"Your father seems happy. Don't you think?" Martha said.

Her father had a scotch and was talking to a friend of Martha, gesticulating without spilling a drop. He was definitely on overdrive; Tree knew where Holly had gotten her performing genes.

"Yes," Tree agreed. "He does."

"Good." Martha flicked her golden hair behind one ear, then the other. She loosened a strand on one side, twirled it between her fingers. She tittered lightly. "I hope so!"

* * *

All at once the restaurant felt crowded and stuffy— Tree had to get outside. She walked outdoors for the cool air, then remembered: this was Philadelphia, not San Francisco. The night was still muggy and warm. The light from the restaurant splashed slanted squares onto the sidewalk.

A door squeaked open, a side entrance by the kitchen, and she turned to see her father walk out. He leaned on one hand against the wall, his face down. He was sweaty and pale.

"Dad— you okay?" She walked to him quickly then stopped a few feet away. She wondered if he had drunk too many martinis – if her father, at sixty-three, would throw up at his own rehearsal dinner.

He looked up and forced a wan smile. "Tree. What a relief." He wiped the sweat off his forehead and slicked back his hair. It was greyer than she remembered.

"You sick?"

"No."

Pots and pans clanged from the kitchen. "Want to go sit in the park?" she asked.

He nodded. They crossed the street to Rittenhouse Square,

and sat on a bench in the inner circle of the park. In this small shade of green the size of two city blocks squared, it seemed cooler. A lone cricket chirped in the grass behind them. It was odd how in the city crickets were single. There wasn't the chorus of hundreds as in the suburbs, just this lone voice against the cars and sirens and din of a city night.

Her father leaned his elbows on his knees and rested his head in his hands. "Do you think she'd mind?"

He meant her mother. Tree had been waiting all night for him to mention her, she realized now. "Of course not," she said, and started to cry.

He leaned back and put his arm against the back of the bench, stroked her hair against her neck, the way he would after her mother had died and he'd discover Tree in the porch in the middle of the night. "She told me it was okay. Before she died. She said not too soon because of you girls. Did you know that?"

Tree hadn't. It was just like her mother – to give something up before she had to.

"I told her, No way. I meant it. For fifteen years I meant it."

"Dad—" What did he want from her? Permission? She didn't think she could give it.

Tree wiped her tears and looked at him. He was getting old, her father was. His body, always full and muscular, was looking thinned out, strained.

"I just don't know if I can do it," he said.

It was what she had been wanting to hear all along – all night and all week and ever since she'd arrived in Philadelphia in time for her father's engagement. But as she thought of all the things she'd been wanting to say – she's so different from us, she's so different from Mom – she found it wasn't what she wanted to say anymore. Couldn't anyone feel sure of something these days?

"Then don't."

He nodded grimly.

"Unless you love her?"

"Oh, sure, I do. I mean she's marvelous—" Tree waited for her father to go on about marvelous Martha. She was defensible, Martha was. She was smart and beautiful and probably even kind. "She's not Mom, you know. But I'm happy with Martha – happier. She makes me happy."

Tree nodded as if this made sense. Happy, happier, happiest. Didn't her father want happiest?

* * *

Tree didn't turn on the light when she went into her apartment. She padded up to her bedroom loft and undressed in the milky orange darkness of streetlights and moonlight and night. Happy, happier, happiest. The parsing echoed in her mind. As she lay in bed trying to sleep, she thought of Holly and her director, the lingering possibility of David.

Tree sat up in her bed, picked up her phone and dialed David's number. She remembered it more through touch – the pattern of her fingers on the phone – than the numbers themselves. The ring of his phone was also familiar, like someone's accent. "Tree Leaf," he answered after she said hello. He sounded surprised, and awkward, and glad to hear from her. "Hey there."

"Hey," she said, as if the two of them were thirteen.

"Wait— tomorrow's the big day. How's it going?"

"It was— okay. Dad's, well—" She stopped. She wasn't

phoning about her father. "David. Why are you calling me?" The Peco sign shined over the half-wall of her loft. She walked down the stairs and sat, lit by its brilliance, on the couch. 1:10 A.M. 86°.

"Well, my dear." Bantering, teasing. He was in an up mood. It seemed he was always in an up mood when she needed to talk, as if he'd sense it and pick up a shield. "I believe it was you who just called me."

"You know that's not what I meant."

She wondered what he'd been doing on the other side of the phone connection. Had he been online? Was he sweaty from a run? She could picture him in his grey, cut-off sweatshirt, his scrawny, muscled arm, beads of sweat under the line of his black hair.

"Tree, I don't know. It was weird thinking of you back in Philadelphia, by yourself. We always thought we'd go back together. And here I am. Still here."

"Why did you suggest we elope?"

"I don't know. But I couldn't do it. That morning. But I— I think I made a mistake."

In the silence she heard him breathing – his breath always faster than hers, as if he were always on the run, on the move.

"I think that's obvious." They laughed – at her words, at the sound of their laughter, at how ridiculous it all was.

"Let me come to Philadelphia – take you out on a date. We can start over. Hey, you can introduce me to your father—"

"No. David, no."

It came out like an instinct, quick and deep and clear. She let it sit between them in the thick darkness of the airy connection. Both their breathing became soundless, as if it'd been shocked out of them.

"I don't blame you," he said.

PECO ENERGY. IS HERE. TO STAY. She now knew this Peco message by heart – corporate spin on the company being bought by an out-of-state group. Still, she found the message reassuring. NO DOUBT. ABOUT IT, the sign agreed.

* * *

At church the next morning, Holly and Tree clasped hands as they watched their father and Martha exchange vows, rings, kisses, and be married. Martha looked less gorgeous up there than Tree had expected, older, even vulnerable, as if she'd sensed the conversation between father and daughter, sensed again that life could be uncertain. Tree's father, in contrast, looked young and overwhelmed, as if he were doing this for the first time. Then as if with a stranger's eyes she saw this was an older couple, a second marriage, a second chance.

Their father and Martha kissed on the altar, and as they turned to walk back down the aisle, someone started clapping, another person joined in, then everyone was applauding, cheering, laughing. The new couple, both these cool, poised people, blushed hot red. Was it embarrassment? Excitement? Love? Could it be love?

The Road Taken

1. Promise

She remembered preparing for her wedding as if it were a first, elaborate date. She had stood pliant in ivory lace underwear and stockings that hooked at the thigh as her mother and sisters dabbed her with pencils and brushes and sprays, pinned her hair high and stiff off her neck, revealing freckles and lines from a sunburn she had tried so hard to avoid that summer, all of it designed to show off not just her beauty, but theirs – his as a groom, hers as a bride, their romance. The wedding was the first time she'd dressed without him, and for him, in a long time. For two years they'd woken up together, seen each other in all incarnations of showered and pre-showered and in desperate need of a shower. Preparations for an evening out were no longer made so much for each other as for whomever they were joining that night, for Philip and Greg at work, for herself, trying to suit her mood or improve it. And she'd presumed, as she emerged through the netting and satin of her dress that fell swooshing and crinkling over her head, that this would be the last time she prepared for him in secret, wrapped herself up and presented herself like a gift.

She'd been wrong. She wondered, tonight, what impression she wished to make, as she walked to meet him for their first dinner together since they'd declared it over, since they had filed for divorce and declared all of it over – the fights, the silences, the tears, the lovemaking that felt like love again for a few moments until the tears came even while they kissed, shaking her with an emotion she couldn't identify until later, so much later, as loss. She had no desire to be alluring – she didn't want to kick up any lingering flames. Sisterly – if only she could be sisterly, give him a hard hug, place an extravagant kiss on his cheek, cheerful and friendly and encouraging. If he could just admire her soft cotton dress, white with pale flowers, not for any seductive prettiness he might still see but more for how others might admire her, proud for her rather than aching for himself.

As she walked into her favorite Thai place, he was sitting, upright and too thin, at a table for two, the last few months gaunting his body like he was being pulled taut. He stared straight ahead, not glancing toward the door, his face in profile, the way she'd seen him for years by her side at the movies, in the car, watching TV, lying next to her in bed, solemn as he read, even as he slept. He was fingering a red plastic stirrer he'd taken dripping out of his scotch, scotch once a sign of cheer and celebration but now, a sign he was bracing for her. She felt her stomach sicken and twist, any hope for affection between them crumbling brittle and dry in her chest. Her white skirt tangled in her legs as she walked toward him, waiting for him to look up, wishing she could smile, that she could feel like smiling, that between them they could find some way to recognize things past, some way to feel that it hadn't all been a mistake, some hint of why she'd stood years ago in the humid church garden, shivering in the heat, the sweat on her spine chilling her. She wished she could show him now what used to be so easy to feel, wished they could share without burden, without bearing any weight on the present or the future, some sign that they had stood there with promise, that the mistakes two people make were committed later, not at that moment, not right then, as she felt the grass through her stockings on her toes, as the sleeve of his tux, woolish and silky at once, brushed her arm, as his warm palm folded around her fingers.

He spotted her then, as she was halfway through the narrow restaurant. He lifted his hand a few inches off the white tablecloth in a weak wave then returned to his drink. She wondered what they would talk about when they were finished with 401Ks and bookcases and bills. She could hear herself mentioning their friends' trip to Italy, her brother's promotion, anything to avoid having now the talks they should have had then, the confidences years too late. She couldn't bear them anymore, couldn't take any more flickers of hope. Wasn't it over yet? Would it ever feel over? She squeezed past tables steaming with *pad thai* and *tom yum* and *massaman* that she wanted to stop and sample: sit down with a glass of wine to taste other people's favorites, lose herself in flavors she couldn't yet make out.

2. Midnights

It felt like a call in the middle of the night, when her ex-husband phoned late one Thursday morning. Maybe it was her cold – she would find out she had developed bronchitis the next day – or maybe it was the cold medicine that made it seem, after she hung up, that she had been woken from a dead sleep. She sat in the papasan chair in her still-new apartment, her muscles aching from fever, her body weak. It should be dark out; she should be going back to bed. Or maybe it was his description of his own restless night, the quiet panic, the twisting logic, which she recognized from all those times she had been there to listen – *Honey, what's wrong?* – when she would press her body against his – *oh it's just crap at work* – drape her arm over his chest, tuck her knee near his stomach, as if she could protect him from the world.

Now he had to wait until the next morning to seek her solace, to call and talk out what had ostensibly kept him up all night, his new position at work, the company meeting at which he had said too much – *I told Peter they were wrong about that, fucking wrong* – his voice deep and low, then cracking on certain notes as if he were a teenage boy – *sounds like you were diplomatic as usual* – teasing, laughing at her prickly husband, so quiet and steady and hardworking that he surprised people when he burst out at a meeting in anger or conviction, though they should know he cared, if they knew him at all.

Did they know him at all, her husband? *Ex-husband*, she should say. Before the divorce was final, she used to trip over what to call him when she wanted to tell one of his stories as if it were still one of her own. My friend, an old boyfriend, my soon-to-be ex-husband. After the divorce was final she stopped thinking about which words to use and slipped back into *husband*. She hardly ever caught herself, it came out so naturally. A girlfriend would correct her: *Ex-husband*. Did anybody at work know her husband, glimpse his passion, catch his humor, notice how kind he was or, these days, how sad? Often now he sounded energetic, he sounded up. Yet when they spoke she could feel the sadness between them – *so how are you?* Each felt it in the other.

And so she listened when he called that morning – *I didn't sleep at all last night* – surprised the way she used to be when they were just dating and she didn't know him yet, and frustrated too, because she could envision him beside her in the dark, silent, looking straight up, not talking, not *doing* anything, as if the discipline of staring unblinking at the ceiling could make it all go away. *What's important*, she'd say. *You have your health, you have your friends, you have me*, the list of what matters in life so short, in the end, *we have the cats*. She wished she could repeat it to him now, her trite litany, she wished she could be there in the middle of the night when he woke up wrestling with the wrong demons.

He'd soothe her, too, in those hours past midnight when people ought to be asleep. Though she was the calm one, the non-worrier, she'd have bad dreams that made her moan or speak or sometimes yell out. All she'd remember was waking up to her husband's voice – *Sarah, hey, Sarah* – her heart thumping, his hand on her shoulder, nudging her awake – *Sarah, it's okay*. She didn't know why she was scared, what she'd been dreaming, and she wondered if she yelled out now, if she tossed and turned in the night and never knew.

After they hung up, she remained splayed in the purple

papasan chair that she had always wanted, a teenage indulgence, the only furniture she'd bought for herself when she moved out. She couldn't to find the strength to go into the kitchen to take the Tylenol she knew she needed, that he'd be urging her to take if they were home together, carrying it over with a glass of water and an insistent look. The phone where most of their talks now took place was warm in her limp hands. *You have me.* He didn't, not anymore. She pictured her husband waking up in the middle of the night, no one to comfort him.

3. The Road Taken

It was her fourth date with her friend's colleague, a doctor, also recently divorced, and she knew, as they drove at midnight from her friend's party, that she was attracted to him, that he was attracted to her, which was why he was driving them to his home rather than dropping her off at her apartment. She opened the window to the summer night and let her hand flutter in the whoosh of air. She wondered if he would make a pass at her, how a 46-year-old once married for nineteen years might make a pass, if by now he'd be an expert, or if he'd forgotten how. Maybe he would kiss her in the car before going in, offer her a drink in the living room, sit close but not too close on the couch, kiss her before clinking glasses, kiss her after, his mouth tasting of red wine. Would he undress her? How quickly might he undress her? She thought about these things and didn't think about these things, wanting to be surprised, as she turned up the volume of the Bach violin sonatas he'd put on, regimented and gorgeous.

From the darkness emerged another night, another drive, with her husband— no, just boyfriend then, not even fiancé yet, so long ago had it become. They were traveling to Cape Cod, listening to a skit on public radio on their way to getting engaged. She wasn't sure that David would propose that weekend two weeks before Christmas, but they had looked at rings together a month or so before, self-consciously, not quite admitting what they were doing, finding out they liked the same style, just a solitaire. She didn't know he had a ring hidden in his luggage somewhere, but then again she did know, and he didn't know she'd say yes and then again he did. And the girl in the skit who had moved to New York from the Midwest like everyone on that program always had, the girl was wondering if she should get married, or if it was too Midwestern. She and David laughed harder at the jokes than they would have on another night, giddy with their secret – they were getting engaged – and with the future beyond that, a wedding, a marriage, children and a house, vacations and jobs and a life that would go on and on like the shadows of scrub trees and sand dunes along Route 6. They didn't know yet that you couldn't predict the future.

That future was now, here, riding with this new man to his house, speeding along the parkway that felt like a country road in Cape Cod more than it felt like Washington, D.C., the sunroof open to the leafy darkness, knowing they would make love that night and then again not knowing, knowing he knew and then again didn't know. The mystery made the night more exciting, it didn't feel set, nothing was planned, because they could not know what would happen, not tonight, not ever, and that made her sad as well. Her smallest hope – that they would make love tonight, that it would be lovely – might not come to be. So she released herself to the Bach and the tires spinning pebbles from the road and the way the man she wanted to make love to tapped his fingers in halting halftime to the music, his fingers responding, not his mind, beating the rhythm as the headlights lit the night they were rushing into in quick slices, a few trees, the curving road. Just that.

Acknowledgments

"Before Letting Go" appeared in *Ploughshares*. "The Road Taken" first appeared in *Puerto del Sol*, and the last section in *Exposure: An Anthology of Microfiction* (Cinnamon Press). "The One I Will" was published in *Folio*; "Honour's Daughter" in *Other Voices*; "Other Women" in *Potomac Review*, and "My Life in Dog Years" in *Two Rivers Review*. "Changing Color" appeared in *Enhanced Gravity: More Fiction by Washington Area Women* and *Not What I Expected: The Unpredictable Road from Womanhood to Motherhood* (Paycock Press). My gratitude to their editors for publishing my work.

Three stories were part of the Imagistic flash fiction project, which I co-curate with the painter Paul Edwards. And so a special thanks to the artists for the inspiration their images gave me: Janet Passehl for "Dam", which gave life to "Before Letting Go"; Tig Sutton, who also helped me with the French in "Long Division", brought forth by his two paintings, "Moonrise Over the Thérain Valley" and "The Sun Rises Over the Thérain River"; and Harry Holland, whose painting "Lips" inspired my story of the same name. Readers can view these images on my website: www.caroleburns.com

In Thanks

to many wonderful people: Margot Livesey, who has encouraged and supported my writing in so many ways; Maureen Howard and Stephen Koch, for early support at Columbia; Susie Wild, for being such a fabulous editor; Rich, Rob, Torben, and the Parthian team, for taking me on; Linnea Larsson, for lending me her image as a cover; the MacDowell Colony, the Virginia Center for the Creative Arts, and the Hawthornden International Retreat for Writers, for providing quiet refuge; to the DC Commission on the Arts and Humanities and Arts Council England, for funding support; my family in the US and the UK, for not thinking me completely crazy; and all my friends and writing comrades in arms, including: Janet Passehl, Judy Heneghan, Julian Stannard, Mark Rutter, Nick Joseph, Holly Johnson, Joanna Scott, Philip Gross, Richard Bausch, Mary Kay Zuravleff, Mary Watters, Amy Wack, Kate North, and more!

And – of course – to Paul.

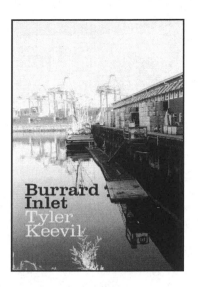

PARTHIAN

www.parthianbooks.com